Praise for *Lorali*

I love Laura's writing. This book turns your brain into an octopus of words.

Gemma Cairney

A fantastic read that is raw, beautiful and bursting with fiercely gorgeous prose.

We Love this Book

It's just as crazy and unpredictable as you'd expect.

The Bookseller

A crash-bang-wallop of vivid storytelling and fun!!!

Nicole Burstein, author of Othergirl

This was the best mermaid book ever!!!

Maddie, Heart Full of Books

Being inside Laura Dockrill's imagination is a wonderful thing.

Jessica, Jess Hearts Books

. . . deliciously bizarre . . .

Kelly, Diva Booknerd

The world Laura writes just begs to be read about and I found myself unable to put the book down.

ibrary

AURABEL

LAURA
DOCKRILL

HOT
KEY
BOOKS

First published in Great Britain in 2016 by
HOT KEY BOOKS
80–81 Wimpole St, London W1G 9RE
www.hotkeybooks.com

A CIP catalogue record for this book is available from the British Library.

ISBN: 978-1-4714-0424-5
also available as an ebook

This book is typeset in 10.5 Berling LT Std using Atomik ePublisher

Printed and bound by Clays Ltd, St Ives Plc

Hot Key Books is an imprint of Bonnier Zaffre Ltd,
a Bonnier Publishing company
www.bonnierpublishing.co.uk

For Daisy and Hector

THE SEA

PROLOGUE

Ah, there you are. Where were we . . .?

'Do you remember anything?' Carmine asked him. She knew more than him; she had watched the young thing grow through the eyes of her Walker friend, Iris. Gutted to see him here now.

It had been a year exactly since the waves stole his soul and drowned him. Carmine had thought, ambitiously, that the date might've meant something enough to stir up a response in the boy.

But he was lost in the wooden maze of the petrified forest; borrowed by both Mer and Walkers, taking turns to disguise itself; a damaged, desolate, barren land for Walkers when my waters washed away only to awaken the sleeping beauty: a tranquil, tropical paradise for Mer to roam and remember.

The boy let his fingertips brush the soft faces of forest trees. Carmine trusted the trunks for contact; let impressionable nature behave as an empty canvas, a love letter, a dial-up telephone.

'What are these marks?' he asked at last.

'They are conversations, memories.' Carmine had to let him explore it himself, discover in his own time. She could lead him to the salt-tear-slicken wrapped letters and notes pinned to the trunks, the engravings. She plucked a silver quill from the tree. It came away with a click. But she couldn't say any more. It wasn't her place. Even though she had seen Iris walk with the boy many times before, even though he was friends with his grandson, she had watched him grow. He was no stranger to her. But she had to pretend they were.

So she circled the trunk, knowingly carving lettering of her own. The boy watched, curiously; he'd never seen any Mer do this before.

'Conversations with who?'

'With who we were; those we left behind.'

'Behind?'

Had she said too much? He was too young. His tapestry was as white as the moon and as blank-faced too: unformed and premature.

I was beginning to wash away, level and become shallow, my tide crawling backwards. It was time to leave; soon this wouldn't be a place for them.

'We can come back, another time perhaps?'

'Will you bring me back though? I won't be able to come alone.'

This didn't surprise Carmine. Zar was extra-protective over him. But the boy was right to find the forest magical and enchanting, even if he couldn't engage fully with its purpose yet. 'Of course,' she said, although it was hard to hide her disappointment, 'we can come back.'

And so they left. Carmine's heart panged. Soon he would be resolved and then it would be harder. She was so certain he would have felt a tug. Make sense of the miracle as moments flickered back like seeds of a dream in a hurricane.

Carmine would just have to be patient.

But that night, in the clutch of his bed, as he waited for sleep to capture him, he thought he once knew a girl. He once knew the feeling of something different. Something he wasn't feeling here. The tactile recall of wallpaper on his fingertips. Of hot food in his stomach. Of, maybe, scribbly white noises coming from a grey box. Of the grip of tracks under the carriage of a metal train. Of headphones. Of coins in his pockets. Of white smoke in his lungs. Sugar rushing in his blood. The girl came back again; he could almost replay her laugh, the way she leant on him; it was like she was present now, hanging over him like a dense fog. And he stole himself out of his bedroom, snuck away in the midnight darkness, back to where Carmine had taken him.

To the petrified forest. Its towering limbs of bark.

He wove through the labyrinth, lost, his heart pounding. He had to act quickly, before he forgot the feeling and let go of the hunch. But the forest seemed to only encourage the encounters, inviting him to dance with a history. He thought of the beach. Of an older woman with the same blood as his, smiling at him like she knew how to love him . . . Of . . . wait . . . that girl again . . .

He wasn't afraid, even though she was a spirit. Even though she came back to him like a memory. He chased the ghost of

3

her through the trees, a game of hide and seek. Her laughter ricocheted from trunk to trunk. He laughed too, raiding the woods for the little twinkle . . . *Who are you? Why do I feel like we've met before?* But it felt like a cruel joke. Every time he got close to the girl, she vanished. Teasing. He looked like one of those stupid cats trying to snatch at the small yellow circle of light shining from a torch.

It was not real. It was a trick. But he wouldn't be disheartened. No, he had to ride this wave.

What if he never got this feeling again? What if he never got this chance again?

And so with the quill, as Carmine showed him, right there he pressed his hands firmly into the wood, just like Carmine did. Scratching his way in and, as hard as he could, he etched the words into the trunk.

I REMEMBER.

But something was watching him. A shadow. Up behind him. Creeping closer . . . lurking, the sinister smile of something sneaking up his spine. The thoughts were slipping away but the fear . . . He dropped the quill and fled, dashing and darting around the standing spikes as fast as his learning tail could whip. The chase of something after him, quick, *snap*, *snap*, *snap*. Fear, panic, caught hold of him, strangling in the throttled clutch of whatever hand was behind. Terrified to look back.

'KAI!'

The shadow lifted. The chase stopped. Whatever was behind him had rushed away, as a field of blinding yellow tumbled dramatically from the beacon of the octopus search lantern.

Kai smashed into the chest of his father, the king. He looked angry.

'What did you do?'

'Nothing,' he lied when his mouth could form a small sound.

'You are *never* to come here again.'

And he didn't. He never came back.

And neither did the memory of the girl he once knew.

And it was then that Zar decided to sever off the lifeline to the past, by closing the petrified forest for good and taking their memories with it.

And another year passes . . .

We grow with many moons and changing suns. The shift of seas moving, grooving with the minute of a day, the taste of a breath, the climbing of a moment. The closure of the forest allows the unknown wilderness to mark its name. Bold emptiness hogs the boggy marshland, silence crawls, the teeth of hungry monsters lurk.

Habits behave as a clock face in this timeless ocean and another year makes it two years since the boy was given to me; two years now since he was stolen from his walking world.

PART I

AURABEL

AURABEL

'Morning!' I wave to the faces as I rush about Tippi. Got three fish hooked on my hip, a jug of sea-cow milk and a sweet wedge of sap for breakfast.

'You need a haircut, Aurabel!' Titi shouts as she scrambles up her Merbies. 'It's too long now.'

'Never! No such thing as *too long*!' And I throw her a fish. 'Here, feed the babs.'

'Oh, Aurabel, you spoil me.'

'Oi!' cries Orina. She's lounging on her decking, organising the plans for tonight's meeting. 'Chuck us a fish then.'

'You know where the fish are!'

'Don't be tight, Aurabel!'

'Don't be lazy, Orina!'

'It's not laziness, Aurabel, some of us just don't quite have the stamina you do. It's honestly like your tapestry has an engine hidden inside of it!'

'It's all me!' I wink.

'See you at the meeting tonight?'

'For sure. I've got an idea about how to use them shipping containers that dropped into the west. Could make a play centre for the Merbies, and was also thinking we could make a gallery, you know, for all the pictures we have – we could hang them on the walls . . . open it up, like an exhibition, could be fun, nice to share all the images, as inspiration, a bit of culture, something to do?'

'I love it. What a great idea. You'll fancy yourself for position of mayor!'

'Dunno about that.'

'Keep going the way you are.'

'Stop trying to wrangle a free fish,' I joke cheekily.

'I wasn't . . . but if you're offering . . .'

And I can't help but throw her one too.

'Love you!' she shouts after me.

My morning swim is my favourite swim of all. Throwing myself about my town where I know the names. This Tippi town is my home. We're a poor place. Where *we* all live. Where *they* don't. Closer to the Walkers. Closer to the beasts. In this sunken trench, still a way away underneath. Right before where the seabed stops the rocks begin, scooping back up like a hangnail. It's all right though, we don't complain. Even though we got shit vegetation because we can't hardly grow any crops or nothing and they've taken all the males from us. All male Mer get to live in the Whirl. Or, the ones worth keeping, I guess.

Precious males.

SNORE!

EUGH! Drop me RIGHT out! I don't even know what the big deal is. They're only good for one thing, if you ask me. And they can't even do that half the time.

I'm talking about hunting, by the way.

If you didn't know, Mer are a male-deprived species. To most of us it don't make no difference – there's plenty of Mer to make a mate or tessellate with, like, for company and whatnot. If you wanted a male mate, you could salvage, but salvaging is costly, especially for a Tip – just another mouth to feed. Plus then you gotta raise the bloody thing, train the dead human up to be Mer before you can even begin to think about touching tongues with them. That's really time consuming. So only the superior in the Whirl can do that salvaging business. And even then, they encourage mostly male salvaging, really, because there's a shortage. Sure, we were all salvaged once upon a time, long ago, before those in the Whirl got richer and we got poorer and life got harder, and so now we don't. I've never wanted a male, to be honest. Nothing they can give me I can't give myself. See, in Tippi, none of us has 'parents' for one reason or another – ours either left us for dead (realising we weren't quite as special as they thought we were when they salvaged us) or died themselves. So, yeah, down here, we're a pack. A pack of wild Mer that have made our own family out of the scraps we got. Orphaned off into this town as outcasts. We got to make do, as most of us just have what we came with: nothing.

Our terrain is a raving splatter of clutter, of mismatched imbalanced wonky-tonk ripples and riddles of buildings all chancing themselves as make-do homes for us Tips. We're a very competent bunch. Built ourselves gardens and a dump. And we help each other too. Like, if someone has a problem with their slam, one Tip will always try to help another. It's just the way down here. But don't get me wrong, like, we're not soppy. Or weak. Mer are an alpha species and it's definitely survival of the fittest. You have to be a bit like that in Tippi. There isn't always enough to go round, see.

Most slams are shacks all stacked up in blocks, cages covered in rags, odd ends of crates and skips and trucks and all sorts arranged as shops and markets and homes. It's a buzzy little place, sky-high and crowded. We all build close together in these tight little stitches, see – keeps us safe and we like to hear each other, like if danger comes or whatnot.

In the middle of Tippi there's this grand square. It's there we have a meeting point; that's where the fallen plane is. Surrounding that, we have the crops that we *can* grow here, which aren't many, as I said – we don't get as much light as the Whirl does and it's pretty boggy down here but we got roots and some of them sprout flowers, which are well pretty; even though they aren't that great to eat, they still look nice.

My slam is an upturned car. Some of the idiots round here think that cars are meant to be that way. Driven that way up there on land. Like, with the wheels in the sky. IDIOTS. Course that ain't how they use them. You don't even have to know about *Walkers* to know that. Just plain common sense. It's just how my slam landed. It didn't have a dead body in it or nothing. Some of the others in Tippi who live in cars say that's the real downside about making a car your slam – sometimes there's a

12

Walker who's gone and died in it. You have to pull them out. Bury them, I guess, if you're a nice, decent type. I would. But mostly they'd be fish food by then anyways.

Murray, my girl, is working at the Findings Warehouse today, which is one of the projects that I invented. The warehouse is basically an old fallen ship; inside we keep all the things that fall from the surface, from them Walkers. Obviously we don't always know what is what. What is useful. Valuable. Precious. So we have a system.

We have the Pickers. These are the Tips that route the whole of Tippi, collecting up any findings. Now, this can be *anything*, from remote controls to wardrobes to rope to magazines to food to money. See, we know money to Walkers is like well important, but to us it's meaningless – we get more use out of a bottle top. Funny that, ain't it? Mostly the Pickers just preserve our area, keeping it safe and clean, but if we need something like . . . say, a bit of scrap metal or something we don't have, it's the Pickers' job to go find it. Then, the Sorters are based at the warehouse and they sort through all the findings. It's important that stuff gets sorted properly, like plastic bottles . . . we have tons of them. So we make use of them: floats, furniture, storage. The Sorters also need to be pretty up to scratch on their Walker knowledge because obviously new things come down all the time . . . And these days they are becoming less useful as Walkers rely heavily on technology, so everything is wires and small and shiny and not that useful to us. Was much better before when everything was more manual. Opal used to know lots more than me about Walker objects but she's not here any more so we have to mainly guess.

13

Murray is a Sorter. I think that's the best job of all because it's the most exciting; cleaning grit off a photograph to reveal the chubby smile of a happy Walker baby. It's mostly a nice job. It suits Murray. She gets a real buzz from it. Murray is not her real name, by the way, but we call her Murray because once she found this badge in the Whirl that fell from them Walkers. A little white plastic thing. I mean, I can't read no Walker talk but Opal helped us understand it (before she went up *there* and never came back). She can read but not write in Walker. And she said the small bit in the colour red said, 'Every Little Helps . . .' and then it said the word 'MURRAY' in big letters. She says it's a name badge. So we all started calling her *Murray*. Just sort of stuck, I guess.

I still fancy her every time I see her. Her beads and chains all around her neck; the coloured gems she decorates her arms and head with. Her goofy little thoughts. I like the moments when she pretends she doesn't know that I'm watching her – it's like our tiny secret unspoken game. Just doing her sorting with delicate fingers, her hair wrapped in buns, her purple eyes looking for all things new. And me, just watching, wondering how she fits into the world without me.

My half-moon.

And then she looks up.

Just like that.

And I know it.

Every single time.

THE SEA

HEAVY THE HEAD

Bingo, the sea-monkey butler, awkwardly hands out crusts of sea-biscuit to have with the nettle tea. They hadn't expected guests and so they weren't quite the fancy nibbles the council were used to. Still, it would do to help wash down the matter in hand.

Myrtle, firm but friendly, tries to make a moment's small talk, commenting on the garden's thriving whilst council members Carmine and Sienna sit in chairs and pet the pups, waiting for Zar and Keppel to *finally* come down from their chambers.

'We shouldn't have come,' Carmine whispers.

'It's too late for that. We're here now,' Myrtle whispers back.

'He's had more than enough chances,' Sienna adds bitchily. 'If anything, this meeting is *overdue*!'

'Precisely!' Myrtle murmurs out of the corner of her mouth before enthusiastically greeting Keppel as she drifts into the garden. Her guards of narwhals stalk busily behind her, tusking and clattering, loyally marking her every move. She is grey; worn down. Her tapestry is dried out and veiny. Bruised, almost.

'Keppel, you look tired.' Myrtle holds Keppel to her chest. 'We hate to see you like this.'

Keppel allows herself to be held by her dear friend but she is still full of resentment. Heartbroken, still, for her missing daughter, grieving her own crown. She is an outsider in her own home. The cracks are too big to heal. It hurts her pride that she has lost her seat to a man. Even if that male is *good*. Even if that male is hers. Keppel is too bitter and could not forgive, no matter how many times Zar reminds her that he only took the crown to keep it in the family and save it from going to another council member. (It was no secret that Sienna quite liked the idea of ruling the kingdom herself.) But it didn't make a difference. Keppel rarely comes down from her chamber any more, smoking, drinking, pickling herself in a sour brine of deteriorating, sinking sadness.

Keppel lights the soft ashes of her own pipe before Bingo can get to her, and the king enters the garden. Two chairs remain: an outside throne for the king for meetings such as this and a regular garden chair. Zar sits on the latter. Myrtle can't help but make a point.

'Am I supposed to sit on your throne?' Myrtle addresses the king, hands on hips, even though this is no way to speak to one.

'It's just a piece of furniture, Myrtle.'

'Pardon my brazenness, but it isn't *just* the furniture that's vacant, is it, Your Majesty?'

Myrtle sits, squeezing her plump, swelling hips into the rickety garden throne, her fullness only reinforcing her clout, enhancing her attractiveness. She is a wet rose: flamboyant, heavy and beautiful. But just like a rose, she can be thorny-tongued and needs to be handled with care. The other mermaids seem only to flourish in her surrounding, rising to the stakes, flowering about her, propping her up as if garnishing her like a bouquet.

Meanwhile, Zar crumples pathetically at his weakness, worming his way inside himself like the maggot he feels he is amongst such intimidating, pretty, wild fruits. Visibly crushing. It is painful to know his mate is slowly strangling herself with her own ego. Unable to even look him in the eye in front of the formal wreath of the council.

It is awkward. Carmine shuffles to break the tension, looping her hair around a finger, taking the candy-pink curls down to softly frame her face.

Sienna's eyes are fixed on the king, waiting for the coward to speak.

Myrtle focuses on Keppel. Keppel puffs on her pipe, inhales, exhales, and finally says, 'So what do we do?'

'Oh, I see you'll speak now, in front of *them*?' Zar snaps.

'What are you *talking* about? *You* don't speak to *anybody* except Kai.'

'Please don't bring Kai into this.'

Keppel inhales again, spirals of silver smoke making halos that speak of her thoughts: that Zar had salvaged too soon after Lorali's disappearance. Two years of anger simmering and the wound is not healing. Lorali was their daughter and here he was fathering some new boy. But the thoughts never crystallise into words, just evaporate like the grey ghost that dreamt them up in the first place, moving her further away from Zar and even further from her reality.

Myrtle intervenes. 'Kai is a good point.' Here, Zar can't help but check that Kai isn't around. He would hate for him to hear himself being talked about. 'Of course, we all know you have salvaged a great young male there. We are all aware that after his resolution he *could* make a great king. It would be fantastic if you could keep the crown in the family; I know it's something Netta would've wanted.'

Keppel wants to laugh. Wants to blurt out like she has done many times before, and scream that Kai was not *her* salvage. That no, it probably wouldn't be what her mother wanted at all. To see any *male* in power. Least of all one who had *replaced* her daughter.

Myrtle continues. 'But the way things are going, you are at high risk of losing your crown.'

'They all hate me, don't they?' Zar volunteers miserably.

'I wouldn't say *hate*. That's a very strong word. Just angry.'

'Angry why?'

'You know what they're like, Zar. Tips like the traditional way of doing things; they can be very sexist. We knew crowning you would be a risk and that it would take time.'

'OK, so can't we just give it a bit more time?'

'When we appointed you, we did talk about a few things you would do as king, *promises* – do you remember?'

'Sort of . . . ish.'

'None of them have been fulfilled. The Mer are disappointed, frustrated.'

'You're too lenient and forgiving,' Sienna adds. 'You're not firm enough with them. They will eat you up alive!'

'I think what Sienna *means*, Your Royal Highness, is that you're too *nice*,' Carmine chuckled, blushing. 'You're just a very nice king and a nice king doesn't always make . . . a good king.'

'Weak is what he is!' Keppel adds as though he isn't there. *Well said.*

'Keppel! Don't say that,' Zar defends himself. 'I'm not weak, I just don't see why I have to baby them all. Surely they don't need *policing* the entire time?'

'You haven't been to visit Tippi once since you've reigned!'

'I've been busy. Raising Kai, the future king! Keppel, don't laugh.' Zar runs his hands through his hair. 'What more can I do?'

'Ah well, this is one of the reasons we wanted to speak to you. You could resolve Kai. A celebration is just what the Mer need.'

Zar shakes his head. 'He's still so young.'

The council want to laugh in the face of this waif. It has been two years since the boy was salvaged, but he is treated like a baby.

'I think it would help. It would cement you as king; to salvage is commendable, it reflects strength. It will give the Mer a chance to get to know you. I think the Mer would like that.'

'I don't know.'

'It's just a suggestion,' Carmine comforts. 'We're only trying to help.'

Zar chews his lip. The reason he has put off resolving Kai is because it would mean he is fully grown. Independent and out of his grasp. Zar isn't sure that is what he wants this time round, not yet anyway. And what would his tapestry say? What if the resolution unveils a new darkness; what if Kai wants to leave him too, like Lorali did?

'You know once he resolves, it will be harder for him to leave you, don't you?' Sienna, as if reading his mind, reassures him. This is true. Surfacing is close to impossible once a Mer has resolved. Zar throws a look to Keppel, her glassy eyes – how he wants them to shine at him once again like they used to. Perhaps letting go of Kai a little would make space in Keppel's heart for him again. 'All right, we can do it. We can resolve Kai.'

'Bravo!' Myrtle claps. 'That will cheer the Mer up! And us, of course!'

'Anything to make this role a little easier. Who knew the public were so *demanding*?' the king groans, managing to force an exhausted smile.

'I wouldn't say they are exactly demanding, Zar; you've done your best to neglect them,' Keppel chips in.

'*Neglect?* I protect them, don't I?' Zar defends.

Myrtle interrupts. 'You protect them, yes. We know your heart is in the right place but closing the petrified forest did not go down well.'

'I closed the petrified forest, Myrtle, because it's dangerous. Walkers know about us now; have you forgotten that?'

'And what about the Mer? About their happiness – have *you* forgotten that?' Myrtle argues back. 'You're just being selfish over your boy – you don't want Kai to remember who he is, where he is from! You can't control that, Zar! It's close to impossible that he will ever remember anything at all! Access to the forest is a privilege to all Mer!'

The taboo topic of memory is rarely discussed amongst council members – it is too personal, too emotional. Carmine stares at the king hard now; she is the only Mer who has managed to successfully contact her past, summoning a dialogue between her oldest and truest friend, Iris.

'You're right, Myrtle: he doesn't want Kai to remember.' Keppel turns to face her mate. 'You don't want him to remember anything, do you, Zar?' Her voice softens. 'And I understand that. We lost Lorali because she wanted to remember and look where that left us. I can see why Zar doesn't want Kai to go.'

Carmine feels sick. She wants Kai to know who he is. That he is missed and loved. She hates that he has to be raised in this hostile environment, with Keppel and Zar snapping at the seams. He deserves better. She wants the forest to be opened immediately. She wants Kai to speak to Lorali, before he is resolved, before it is too late, so that he might be able to try to go back. But she doesn't have the guts to say, and so respectful is she of the laws of the forest she couldn't say even if she tried to.

'But the forest is too dangerous now. It's full of beasts and monsters.'

'That's because it's been left to fend for itself. We have to begin using it again and reopen it. We can do it safely.' As keeper of the beasts – the ones they *could* keep, anyway – Sienna bites back in defence of them.

'If I open up the forest, will that warm them to me?'

'I think it would.' Myrtle nods. 'It's a basic right.'

21

'It will take work.'

'Yes, but Sienna can take her monsters there, clear the site – can't you, Sienna?'

'Certainly – my lot can do their best to starve out whatever beasts are squatting.'

'And then we can invite the Mer along? To a grand opening? Involve them?' Zar's voice begins to lift.

'I have an even better idea,' Sienna suggests, all ears pricking up. 'One that will make a real impact.' It is rare that Sienna has suggestions at such meetings. It isn't that she's not sparky or interested, she just can't be bothered to waste her ideas on the council. Her collaborative streak is one the others rarely get to see. 'We should employ a Tip. Zar should enrol one of the Tippi Mer to represent the forest. Somebody who can spearhead the opening.'

'Like a ranger?'

'How wonderful!' Carmine claps.

'Employing a Tip? But we've never done that before!' Myrtle is concerned.

'It *would* make an impression.' Keppel nods.

'It's the ultimate way to reconnect.'

'Why don't we gather a few of them? We could employ a team; get the community spirit going,' Zar suggests.

'Perhaps eventually, but knowing the Tips I think that one will make more of an impact, more of a statement,' Sienna argues.

'They are so competitive, those Tips,' Myrtle replies. (Which was *rich* if you ask me, but anyway . . . my lips are zipped.)

'A bit of friendly competition has never been a bad thing.' Sienna grins. 'It would certainly put a sting in their tail.'

MERMAID AND MERMEN APPRECIATION TRIBE – aka 'MAMAT'

This site is dedicated to the memory of Charlotte Wood. R.I.P. We luv u babe. We wil NEVA 4GET U. U wil ALWAYZ remain a REAL mermaid in r eyes. <3 <3

YOOOOOO!!!!!!!! We hve jst reached 1 million subscribers. We LITERALLY cannot believe it! DYIN!!!!!!!!! I am so excited I can't even rite. I am shaking. Jst so proud becuz I remember starting this and everyone thinking I was crzy and tht I'd lost the plot like . . . MERMAIDS – WOT? WTF? And now 2 hve 1M of Us lot is jst a JKE! Jst shows how far we've come! YYYYYYYYYPPP! ILY! ROLF! LOL! DYIN! FANX so much. I luv U all so badly. I'll rite a new post when I've calmed down frm the HYPE! Check insta for pics. BRB.

MermaidFanGirl_1: OMG! 1M! Holy moly! Since the start, until the end. MAMAT is the reason I live. Love you @MerBaby3000

Vampfish: ILY! ILY! ILY!

TwistedTail2: WHAT THE ACTUAL F***! Does Opal Zeal no this tho? 1 million! Jjjjjeeeeeeeeeeeeeeeeezzzzzz . . .

MerBaby3000: Awwww @MermaidFanGirl_1 you're the best. Orige Mamat crew! Luv u beb xxx

WhereisLorali: I CNT believe this! I am LICKING THE SCREEN. MY MOM THINKS I AM CRAY CRAY BUT I DON'T CARE!

Vampfish: Course Opal nos bebz, Opal follows!

TwistedTail2: GASSSSSSSED! BRAP BRAP! ****GUN FINGERS*** YA DUN NO!

MerBaby3000: @TwistedTail2 ☺ ☺

OPALGUSH: No bt Opal don't evn look afta her own twitter accnt so . . .

URSULA_8_LEGS: @OPALGUSH U DON'T KNOW THAT 4 SURE.

Bellaseashella: BTW GUYS my dad says he heard Lorali lives in Iceland.

OPALGUSH: @URSULA_8_LEGS errrr everybdy nos that her PR rites her tweets so hush your gums m8.

URSULA_8_LEGS: @OPALGUSH how bout I am NOT ur mate tho. Soz ☹

OPALGUSH: Whtevs.

CoralCaroline: Iceland? @Bellaseashella total bullshit.

SHAUNTHEPRAWN: @Bellaseashella **BOOKS FLIGHTS TO ICELAND**

Bellaseashella: @CoralCaroline my dad works for a newspaper and said they saw her and tried to interview her but she has some legal restriction thing in place so they can't talk to her. Or ask questions or anything. But it's defs her.

LORALIMYBAE: As IF she'd be in Iceland. What ON earth she doing there? IT'S FROZEN!

TwistedTail2: @LORALIMYBAE innit tho. Ain't no boys in Iceland ☹

CoralCaroline: @LORALIMYBAE most probably hiding from psychos like you.

HDDNTRSRE: @CoralCaroline LOLZ

MermaidFanGirl_1: @CoralCaroline we've reached 1M followers 2day can u jst not start beef w nebdy 2day plz? FML!

CoralCaroline: SICK to death of everybody on this dumb forum, stop harassing Lorali, can't you lot take a hint? You're like a bunch of stalkers. Just leave her be. It doesn't matter where in the world she is because it's NONE of your business, just let her get on with her life. AND GET A LIFE yourself.

Vampfish: She probably doesn't even have a passport anyway.

MermaidFanGirl_1: @CoralCaroline if u h8 it SO much then dnt cme here, ur alwz so disrspctful.

THEREALOFFICIALOPALZEAL_37: @CoralCaroline you have been throwing your negativity round here for years now. It's not on. Stop it right now.

WhereisLorali: @MermaidFanGirl_1 UR RITE. @CoralCaroline moans bout us lot being stalkers bt she's jst as bad, on here every day jst like us, if u dnt like it go find some dry squad 2 go b a part of bt dnt mug us off.

SHAUNTHEPRAWN: @CoralCaroline has a point. It's all slightly sycophantic.

CoralCaroline: I only come on here to laugh at your ignorance.

THEREALOFFICIALOPALZEAL_37: @CoralCaroline bully!

LORALIMYBAE: Wot does sycophantic mean please tho?

WhereisLorali: It's no wonder Lorali has mvd to Iceland wen she's got fans like U!!!!!!! @CoralCaroline

FLLWMELORALI: She's not in Iceland. She's in London.

L-O-P-A-L-I: Mebbe she's up in Florida. That's where I would be.

Vampfish: @L-O-P-A-L-I nice user name <3 <3

L-O-P-A-L-I: @Vampfish fanx :D

WhereisLorali: Whereva she is she obviously don't wnt 2 no us and it's breakin my heart I am literally CRYING my actual REAL LIFE eyes out so hard all u lot fink this is a jke bt this is actually like my REAL actual life. I hve waited 4 so long 4 a chance 2 meet her and it hurts me so much to know she's out there sumwhere in the world and I can't just tlk 2 her. EVERYBODY knows what a mermaid fan I am, I am like literally obsessed.

MermaidFanGirl_1: @WhereisLorali awww bbz dnt cry. One day you'll get the chnce to meet her, stay positive.

LORALIMYBAE: We are ALL mermaid fans on here actually @WhereisLorali n we ALL love Lorali, not just u, stop making it abt URSELF the WHOLE time.

WhereisLorali: I am not saying we aren't. But I am defo the biggest Lorali fan in the whole world.

Bellaseashella: @WhereisLorali I am too!

WhereisLorali: No offence @Bellaseashella but her name isn't even in ur user name so . . .

LORALIMYBAE: I am a WAY bigger fan, ask my brother.

WhereisLorali: I suffa from depression and anorexia and I like literally have no friends and I have that torrets thing that when you speak only mermaid fings come out my mouth and it's so embarrassing. THAT'S how big of a mermaid fan I am.

Vampfish: SORRY NOT TRYNA BE RUDE OR NAMING ANY NAMES BUT REMIND ME WHAT ANOREXIA HAS GOT 2DO WITH MERMAIDS? *cough cough* ATTENTION SEEKING!

HDDNTRSRE: Ha! Innit tho! SO tru! LOLZ! @Vampfish

Bellaseashella: @WhereisLorali I go swimming 3 times a week.

WhereisLorali: @Bellaseashella ha! Dnt mke me laugh, like how old r u? Like 12? 3 times a week is nothing! So babyish. Sometimes I look down and my legs are turnin in2 a tail, the skin is actually attaching, I ain't evn jking.

Vampfish: @WhereisLorali Sure that ain't just fat?

HDDNTRSRE: @Vampfish LOLZ!

WhereisLorali: NO IT IS NOT FAT! And that's actually a very insensitive thing to say to somebody with a sickness. Lorali is my actual queen and when SHE'S ready 2 b MY friend then we will have sleepovers and be best friends 4EVA and u lot will really know then who her MAIN fan is.

CoralCaroline: DEAD.

Iso_fairy_dust14: Hi guys, what does everybody think about fairies?

Lorali

I REMEMBER

The scrambling yawn of the hoover cricks off and I take a moment to adore the silence. Moments like this catch me – happiness – when I look about Iris's charming shop of bric-a-brac. The pieces of history and memory all there waiting patiently to be rehomed and loved again, on to make more history, more memory. Many of these belongings outliving their first loves. There is always an excuse to get lost in the crispy spine of a sun-stained atlas, be frozen inside the brassy eye of a telescope, hunt nostalgia hidden in the damp, rotting, musky fabric of an ancient hand-woven rug.

I catch my reflection in the back of a spent silver spoon. My eyes are a more purple-green now that seem to match the rainbow spoil of a polluted gutter. My hair an ashy blonde. Like dust. Long and up in a loose knot. I am so simple, I think. In my basic cream jumper and light blue jeans. Flynn got me these trainers. Beaten-up rubber pumps. They are white with a star on them. They are so comfortable. I wear them every day. I see girls in town. With painted eyebrows and lashings of mascara. Girls who show off their bodies and mix up the colour of their hair. Wear treasure. But not me. Cheryl says I should go out more but it's not for me. I wouldn't know how to begin making any new friends. Still, it doesn't stop people staring in the foggy town of Hastings. At my eyes. Like I'm an animal they want to touch but are afraid of. And that's why I stick here, shying away, in the shop.

We've worked so hard on the place. Flynn and I. Many late nights with the old records and the sparky purr of electric heaters to get things ordered and priced properly. I mean, money still sometimes goes over my head but Flynn seems to know what is what and if he doesn't we just make a price up, and if we *really* like something, like the rocking horse, for instance, we make the price so outrageous that nobody would ever buy it anyway, and if they *did* we'd make enough money for the shop that we could buy *hundreds* of rocking horses.

We even have *customers* now. At first they were mostly press and reporters. Horribly intrusive, bargy people with cameras and notebooks asking me questions and pushy agents offering me deals and sometimes it was strange people with staring starry eyes all glued up to my face, but now it's just *people* people. Antique people, bargain hunters, browsers, tourists. Real-life people who just think I'm a normal person like them, working in a shop. Walkers. I can't believe how long I've been here. My own dust added to the windowsill, my fingerprints on the glass, my strands of hair in the carpet.

Old Iris pads down the ladder from the lighthouse, being the huge wardrobe-sized person that he is. Sometimes I capture him, in a certain moment, in the wrong light, and become totally aware of how old he actually is. His wrinkles folded like ripples of sand tracing the tide, sweeping lines of stories. But it's in the last year that his age has really shown and he's begun to slow, a painful reminder that we aren't immortal. That he's just a human. Just like me.

It's been a year since Carmine inexplicably stopped making contact. The side effects of withdrawal are shrinking him.

'He still not back with the cake yet?'

It's what Iris and I both have in common. We like to have huge slabs of cake in the afternoon. Carrot, chocolate, Victoria, coffee; we love it all. Rich, smooth, creamy icing and light, forkable sponge. With tea, which I drink now – can't believe it. I'm a tea drinker. That's Cheryl though. She drinks so much tea. And we do here too. I've learnt it's something to do when you don't know what to do.

'No, he has been a while, hasn't he?' I peer out of the window. The sea shushing in and out. Summertime in beautiful Hastings. A nearly blue sky. The 'V' of winging birds. Sad it's almost done.

'The tea'll be all spotty; I don't like it when it gets that brown stuff on top,' Iris moans, which is a lie. His tea has brown spots on it all the time. Matches the patches and ageing spots on his head. 'And I don't even fancy cake any more – he's been so long, I've gone off the idea!' More lies from the old man.

We've changed the name of the shop to Iris Spy. Because Iris is known for his magic eyes and these are his findings; all this stuff that he's collected and found over the years.

'Should have called the shop Iris *Lies*!' I laugh and Iris is left trying to unpick my cheap joke. He raises a brow, spluttering into a tea-stained coloured rag. I've told him he needs to visit the doctor. But he won't go. Even though he says he's living on 'borrowed years'. The bell tinkles and here he comes. Flynn. Dumping the brown paper packages on the counter before me, he grunts, knocking his bike to the floor as he charges through the shop and up to the house.

'Oh, *very* pleasant!' Iris remarks with sarcasm.

'Give it a rest, Granddad,' Flynn barks back. 'You're not even meant to be eating sugar.'

Iris rolls his eyes, takes off his glasses and gives them a wipe. 'Strange boy,' he tuts before reaching inside the crumpled bakery bag. 'Oooo look, Lorali, it's Victoria!'

I find Flynn upstairs. Watching TV blankly. His mind in a maze. At eighteen now, his shoulders are wide; he is tall and lanky with long skinny legs that are always covered in bruises. Clear, blue eyes and a long nose. He has a face that always looks like he's apologising.

'Flynn? Are you all right?'

'There was nothing there.'

Dead. For. A. Minute. Trying to make my voice not crack. 'I told you not to go.' We had both promised each other.

Doesn't stop my heart sinking. Hope crashing. I've been riding the days out myself and fighting the urge to go.

'Yeah, well, he's not coming back.'

It has been two years since Rory drowned, or so we thought. A year since Rory wrote 'I remember' on the trunk of a tree in the petrified forest.

I REMEMBER. I REMEMBER. I . . .

We have been back nearly every day since, *all* of us. Flynn and Iris and Cheryl of course. Writing our own messages, leaving our own gifts and stories, and had nothing back. Even Rory's dad came once, all the way from Spain, in hope it would jog his memory. But nothing. We both swore that we'd stop going, that we'd not keep looking, torturing ourselves with the promise of hope. Especially not today – it is two years ago today that he left us behind.

'You don't know that,' my voice rasps. 'You don't remember as a Mer, not unless your tapestry gives something up, shows a certain colour or pattern – there's no way of knowing anything at all otherwise.'

'Or maybe he's just chosen to forget us.'

Flynn wants me to argue that. Or maybe he wants to hurt me, for me to believe that he could have forgotten us. I don't know. I don't know what is going on down there any more. I know as much about the Whirl now as I once knew about this place. And that angers Flynn. Why can't I give him any answers? About the Whirl; about Rory? About where his best friend has gone. And how it is all because of me. That I am here and Rory isn't. Traded places. In the blink of an eye. Flynn now has to have me as a friend instead of Rory. And some days, he just isn't OK with that.

'I'm sorry, Flynn.' I sit next to him on the tired sofa. I link my arm through his. I feel his elbow tense against me, then relax in one move.

'No, I'm sorry. I shouldn't be taking this out on you. I'm just disappointed. I really felt that he'd be there today. All night I just knew it, like he was talking to me.'

'I get the same feelings.' I grip his hand. 'Obviously not the same as yours . . .' I catch myself – Flynn is sensitive. 'But I still feel him around.'

'You don't have to pretend you don't miss him, Lorali. It's so shit. It's like he's dead but he's alive . . . I'm grieving him and missing him but at the same time it's killing me to not know what he's up to, who he's with . . . if he's OK.'

I nod. My eyes make water.

'I shouldn't have put the pressure on myself that today would be the day . . . He might not even know when a year even is? He might not know anything.'

Of course I'd thought about all of this. I had imagined the life Rory would be living underneath in the Whirl. So bittersweet, this notion, of knowing he was salvaged. Salvaged because he is strong. Special. Deserving to be rescued. That he truly is the special person that I'd known him to be. They saw a shine in him. He is one of a kind. The kind who died to save me. A kind I would never get to know again.

Does Rory think about me enough to feel the same? Does he resent me? Miss me? And how much does he remember . . . Does that mean that the Mer know about *me*. That I have surfaced? Here I am living as a Walker. Like some fraud. Wearing shoes and working a job.

My trail of thought is drowned out by Flynn's tapping. 'Look, look, Lorali, look!'

It's Opal Zeal. The 'celebrity mermaid'. On TV. She's being driven around in some sort of bathtub on wheels at some swimming pool or something, the flipper of her tail curving over the edge of the tub. Her hair is twisted up in horns.

'Where is she?' I shake my head in disbelief, dreading to think what she's up to *this* time.

'Looks like she's at a leisure centre or something.'

Dozens of brightly coloured noodle-like tubes loop together in the shot behind her – slides, I guess. During the interview her hairstyle of horns seems to look like slides popping out of her head. If only I could whoosh down one myself and see what was going on in that deranged brain of hers. I can't even see her tapestry with all the make-up and glitter. We don't speak any more. The more the interview goes on with the shots of the park it becomes apparent that this isn't just any water park. This is Opal Zeal's very own water park. To finish, the TV shows where Opal is currently living. Some hotel in central London. It looks like a palace.

'I don't get it,' I can't help but snarl. 'Why would you let these journalists come to where you live? Why would you want the public to know where you are?'

'Publicity,' Flynn shrieks. 'She loves it. Look at all those idiots.' The presenter shows the hundreds of people standing outside Opal's hotel with their cameras and autograph books. Most of them are dressed as 'mermaids' and sea-monsters. Fake tails. Face paint. Wigs. Some look as though they've spent the night there, waiting for her to appear. And when she does, she comes from a car. In sunglasses and a white fur coat. She's in that stupid saltwater bathtub thing again, being lifted by six giant men dressed like undertakers, the fin of her tail flopped over the side, carried like a coffin.

'This is so weird. I don't get it.' Then again there's loads I don't get. I still don't get how we are watching moving images

in real time on a screen that's inside a metal box. That's why I
like the shop. Where things are slow. Or broken. Hidden away.
I'm not sure if it's Opal or the fast-moving images that makes
me feel more sick.

'Yuck. Turn it off.' The room halts to silence.

'So what does she have now then?' Flynn laughs, counting
on his fingers. 'A cocktail bar, night club, nail bar, hair salon
and now this?'

'Errr . . . don't forget the posh sushi restaurant she's opening,'
I add. Which I have to say I find gross, considering she's meant
to be *protecting* the ocean.

'She must be worth a fortune!'

'And her bikini line, her endorsements . . . her beauty range.'
I roll my eyes. I learnt that off Iris.

'The woman's a beast!' Flynn gawps.

'That's one word for it,' I snub.

'Come on, Lozza, let's get you out there – you must be able
to do some of this shit,' Flynn jokes.

'They don't want me with these two things though, do
they?' I shove my feet in his face, wiping the soles all over, my
big toe in his ear. We laugh and Flynn jumps on me: tumbling,
play-fighting, rolling over and laughing. But then Flynn drops
his forehead; he isn't laughing any more. He's sad. I hold him.
He holds me back. Holding on in the absence of the one person
who we both want to be holding. But can't.

AURABEL

BLOOD PEARL

I'm just about the first one awake. I know why it is. I'm too excited. Stretching, I creep out of the slam so as not to wake up Murray. Catch us an eel or two for brekkie. Nothing long. I love it when Tippi is like this. Sound asleep, almost beautiful, almost forgiven.

But I bounce out of bed today because something bloody brilliant has happened ...

I've only gone and got myself a job.

Can you believe it though – me? With a job. And not just *any* job neither. NAH! One for the KING! Yeah, I suppose he is a bit of a pushover for a king. AND it would've been better if it was a real *queen* I'd been working for, you know? I would've loved to have worked under a great like Queen Netta, or even Keppel. That would be a *real* honour. But still. It means I could get outta Tippi. And who knows? If I do well maybe they'll move me up the ranks one day. Get myself promoted – become an adviser? Maybe I'm gonna make something of myself. I know I don't really have the words for it but I know about *stuff*. I keep up with all the politics from over there in the Whirl. And the best thing about the whole thing is this: I am working on the project to reopen the petrified forest. How *wicked* is that? Because the petrified forest is like *everyone's* favourite place – it's where we go to smoke and hang and just chill, really, and when that *king* made it out of bounds, everyone lost their shit. So really, it's two good things in one, a win-win . . . not only is the forest opening again, I'm only the bloody one helping to do it! And everyone is well jealous.

I'm not gonna mess this up like that Opal Zeal. She's a traitor. Rumour is she's working for the government now. Up with them Walkers. Weird in all, isn't it? So dodge.

Shit, I gotta shut up. I gotta get ready for work!

'Morning, star.'

'Eel over there if you're hungry.'

'Yum. Not right now though – just woken up.' Murray yawns. 'You nervous?' she asks sleepily, turning over on the back seat.

'Nah.' I do one of those stressed contagious yawns right back at her. Murray wiggles closer, strokes her hand down my back on my spine. 'I'm fine. I just want to do it right, you know? Don't want to let myself down, Murray.'

'You could never let yourself down.' She crinkles up her nose. 'It's kind of technically impossible; you're just one of them ones that always does life well.' She kisses me on the lips.

I kiss her back.

Raise an eyebrow at her.

Do a stupid face.

Murray laughs. Leans in as her hands creep. My tapestry shimmers in shivers – pastel-chalk pink right up next to powdery turquoise. We once found a two-tone tea set in the sand that looked identical to my tapestry colours. It lay perfectly lined up, the mini plates all exactly aligned, as if stacked on a shelf.

'Oi, not now.'

'Ow!' Murray snatches her walking fingers back as I whack them away, flipping onto the backseat. Her plaits are loose and beginning to unravel.

'I need to look fresh.'

'You always look fresh, Bel. I don't know quite *how*, but you do.' She holds a cheeky grin in. Her hands are in prayer position as she tucks them under her chin and watches me move. In our mirrors I see her. Like a beautiful scribble of colour in the corner of my eye. Shell-shaped eyes. Tattoos scrawled all over her body, only with sea quills so not *forever* ones. All over her shoulders and stomach and entwined around her spine up to her neck are looping, swirling, mad illustrations and splattered patterns. Think they might be inspired by her tapestry but you wouldn't know that because she draws all over her tail in ink too, which she isn't really meant to do but whatever.

'Shut up, you,' I growl.

'How are you gonna wear your hair then?' Murray asks. I'm known for my hair, see. *Weird.* To me it's just hair.

'Same as always. Just like this. And before you *even* ask, *no* make-up. I don't feel myself when I wear it. It don't suit me. I look like a clown fish.'

'I wasn't going to say that!'

'You were!'

'I wasn't!'

She was.

'You don't need make-up, Bel.'

'Here we go . . .'

'No, not *here we go* at all, actually . . .' But she can't help herself. 'I was thinking, you could maybe wear just a little bit? Some gemstones or roses? Just to –' I jump on top of her and tickle her ribs. 'I'm joking, I'm joking!' she squeals.

'You better be!' I snap back up and finish getting ready. I tip my hair down – it brushes the tip of Murray's tail; it's like a waterfall. 'What do I do if I run out of things to say?'

'Let's be serious for a second, please. When does *that* ever happen, Aurabel?'

'What if I get nervous? Or if it's too much?'

'You know what to do, remember?' She closes her eyes and takes a big, deep breath, holding my wrists. 'You just close your eyes, inhale . . . breathe and count, six, five, four, three, two, one . . . and then exhale all your fears and worries away.'

'That counting thing works for you, Muz, but not for me.'

'If it works for me, then it can work for you.'

'No, you're all . . . *hippy-dippy* peace and love . . .'

'So are you,' she argues, almost defensively, like she's arguing *my* case against *me*. She looks at my tapestry; she's into reading them as well, constantly trying to work out how I'm feeling. I turn away from her.

'I'll think of you doing it and then maybe it will keep me calm, how about that?'

41

I feel Murray's eyes tracing my back. 'Can't I come with you? Just for the adventure?'

'No, Muz.'

'Least let me swim there with you.'

'No, it's mad far.'

'Can't I just slip into your hair and hide?' She leans forward again, crushing her face into my neck, pushing my hair up into a bunch, whispering in my ear: 'I'll be as quiet as a starfish.' I push her off. She slumps back into the bed, all moody now – *grumpy sea cow* – but I ain't got time for her pulling one of her moods. 'You don't need to *change*, Aurabel,' she hisses.

'Stop using that *change* word, Murray. I'm not gonna change, I'm not *changing*. I just want to . . . do good . . . get us out of this . . . pile of shit.'

'Pile of shit?'

'I meant it as a joke.'

'Thought you loved our slam.'

'I do.'

'Why'd you call it a *pile of shit* then, Aurabel?' She frowns. 'What's wrong with it?'

'Nothing, Murray, it's just small, isn't it? It's lovely and it's ours but what if one day we want to salvage? Can't do that, no space – we're practically living on top of each other as it is.'

'Fine. I'll go back to my crate. I've still got a bed there.'

'I didn't say that!' I shout. She turns her back on me. I see her eyes looking down. I know it's weird. No one from Tippi ever gets a job. Ever gets anything, really. Murray and me are used to being together. And just yesterday we were young and

42

for ever with no responsibility and now . . . we can't be that so much any more. Cos I got work. Work in the Whirl.

I knew she was worried. She hates the idea of me working there, in the forest, no matter how many times I reassure her that I'll be protected by the royal beasts and that I'll be safe; she just doesn't like it.

Murray looks about my slam. *Our* slam. (But it's mine really.) The things I'm into. Even though they've enveloped around her for all this time; seen them a trillion and one times before. My instruments. The few crappy findings I own. The things she's given me. The beauty she finds in tininess. All the pictures and stuff I like stuck to the metal angles of the vehicle walls. Photos from magazines: nature. Planets. Volcanoes. Hurricanes. Storms. Waterfalls.

She spins about. Her cheeks all rosy, nervous. Her silhouette – the tip of her nose all flat and then dipping up into a peak. Murray's hand clenched up in a tight ball, waiting to surprise me I suppose, because that's what she does next.

'Good luck on your first day at your new job, Aurabel. I'm proud of you.'

She stuffs a little string into my hand and on it is a blood pearl. The most special of all pearls. The blood pearl is formed inside the red oyster, one of the rarest creatures in the water. They say that finding a blood pearl is a miracle because their breed is so uncommon they are almost extinct. And when the blood pearl is formed, the oyster perishes. These blood pearls are deep red. You know pearls are formed from a toxin? Say, a grain of sand gets caught in the oyster flesh, and the oyster produces a protective layer to coat the grain, so it doesn't

43

infect or contaminate the purity of the oyster. Over the years, all of the layers add up and up and eventually make a pearl. So mad to think that something so beautiful can come from an impurity. And my cod, have you ever seen an oyster? They are so bloody ugly. That's the thing about nature – it gives unique beauty to one of the ugliest species.

And here I am holding one. I look up at Murray. 'It can be a bracelet or a necklace, whichever you like better . . .' She admires it. 'Or annoys you the least, I guess. I made it.'

'You made it?' I gasp. 'Why?' I didn't mean to say *why* but it just bounded out of my gob. Cos so beautiful is this little simple thing. All string with its one delicate handsome red bead. I can't believe why anybody, even Murray, who I am closest to, would take the time to make me anything so pretty.

'I wanted to. It will bring you luck.'

'How did you find it?'

'I don't know.' She smiles. 'Luck I suppose.'

So touched. 'I'll wear it as a necklace, because I don't want to lose it now, do I?'

'I thought you would, that's why I made it longer. Here. Let me help you do it up.' Murray turns me round and lifts my hair. 'Bloody hell, your hair is so heavy!' She knots up the back for me. It tickles. 'You'll need the good luck to take this thing off.' She laughs. 'I had to double knot it.'

'Good.' I blush. 'I don't want to take it off.' I feel so important now and safe somehow. I check it out in the wing mirror of the car. It's all shiny and lovely and catches the light of my bluey-green hair and I touch the pearl softly and then I turn to face Murray to see what she reckons. But we catch ourselves

44

in a kiss. Kissing like we are out of breath and the only air we can get is from each other like this. All mad hands in hair and tight grip; can't get enough of the warmth. Squash. Press – restless heat and fluttering of hearts banging out of chests and sliding tongues and hot breath and gentle raw sting, cling, in this moment but tingling all over and my tapestry changing colour – all shy now – as we roll over into the back seat of my car. Scooping. Tumbling, clumsy, shapes of us, reaching, tessellating, fitting, locking, sticking, stuck. But a velvet, soft landing from the women-ness of us, so simple. Fingers. Mouth. Neck. Bound. Knotted up together all nice. Too nice.

Six, five, four, three, two, one.

Six, five, four, three, two . . .

Six, five, four, three . . . Six, five, four . . .

Lorali

THE PETRIFIED FOREST

I said goodbye as normal. Heavy with the warmth of Iris's burnt sausages and creamy mashed potatoes in my stomach.

Even though I know nothing will be there, just like it never is, I can't help myself.

The water is already almost too high. Sinking the forest in the night-time. The salty sea lapping at the bark. But parking my bike, flipping my pumps off and rolling up my jeans, I'm able to walk towards it. Even though the summer air is warmish still, the sea is cold. Needling, wincing and urgent. Every time I step into the sea it feels like the first time, over and over. Reintroduces itself, sniffs me out, like I'm a stranger with a face it will never remember.

The petrified forest; the in-between. I forgot how fortunate I am to be able to know this forest in both of its lights. Stark, bald and desolate to the Walkers – a dark and exciting landscape for hide and seek, climbing and dog walks. But underneath, when it reacts with the salt of the sea, it fruits, blossoming into a bounteous bloom of exotic wilderness and colour.

There are Rory's words. As always. Engraved into the same tree. A year older.

'I REMEMBER'

Nothing new. Nothing added. Untouched. Almost as though the Mer are no longer using it, or maybe my eyes just can't read their messages so well any more.

But something makes me go in further. I touch the stumps and trunks of trees, allowing them to rest in their disguise. Their husky croaks give away no secrets of what they see on either world. My fingers jostle into the grooves of all the places I know. The circles. The words. Flashes of my past. I can hear my small self giggling into the empty claws of branches – and as quickly and as suddenly as those thoughts enter my brain and vanish, a black dart heading for my eye misses me, just, stabbing the tree behind. I scream and slam my mouth closed. I can't see anybody. Nobody at all. Only the water rippling in the shooter's wake. Gulping, I walk towards the arrow. Winged, it comes with a rag. I close my eyes, begging that this is word from Rory. *Something.*

A sharp whistle rings, piercing the moment like a balloon popping. I jump. It's the lifeguard; they have to have them twenty-four hours now after the trouble two years ago. No thanks to me. The flags alone won't do any more. 'Excuse me, miss, the tide is coming in. I have to ask you to come away.'

Scrambling, I lunge forward, almost losing my footing on some craggy clutch of rocks. I snatch the rag from the tree, leaving the spike naked. I unpeel the note and see the words:

'UNDER THE PIER. MIDNIGHT.'

AURABEL

FIRST DAY

The palace is mad big. Pretty. I almost have to pinch myself to remind myself it isn't a dream. All flowers and leaves and wispy water willows, all wild growing but proper cared for. Not like the flowers we have in Tippi. They are just dead weeds there. The gates are tall, proper. Nutty hench things with spikes at the top – I mean, don't stop nobody from floating in the top now though, does it? But it looks impressive.

I breathe. Nervous. *OK, Aurabel. Ring the bell.*

The pups bark. Nervously I roll Murray's pearl in between my fingers. Six, five, four ... *What if they don't like me? Murray was right. I should've worn make-up. Why didn't I wear make-up? My hair is too long. It's gonna get in my eyes – what if I don't ... Calm down ... it's OK ... it's ...* Six, five, four ... *three ...*

Eventually the palace gates creak open and out comes that massive scaled snake, Marcia, the palace guard. My instinct is to slit her throat and shed her skin but I have to control myself because she isn't like the monsters we are used to. Nah, this snake is *groomed*! And *trained*. With manners better than mine probably. She sniffs me out.

'Hiya.' I blush. 'I'm here to see the king. It's my first day.' She breathes me in, her eyes on me, then she sneezes in my face before turning away and slurping back into the palace, leaving the gate open for me to follow. Charming. So maybe her manners aren't so good. I wipe the gunk from my face and close the gate behind me before catching up with her.

Inside the palace is RI-DONK-U-LUS. My cod! The walls are sandstone colour and covered in this print like a turtle's back. Speckled like egg and brushed down, so soft to the touch and deliberate. Everything is curved naturally as though the sea built the walls itself – the windows are all warped and melted-looking. Like big groaning mouths. The light just pours in. It's so bright and echoey. Decadent and grand. The rooms are open, which makes you feel proper safe and relaxed even though it's so large and swallowing. Cave-like bends and arcs; sweet areas filled with sponge and coral and sandbags and cushions to chill out. Pillars hold the floors up, covered in broken mosaic chinks of mirror and stone and shell. Art *everywhere.* Findings everywhere. Murray would LOVE it here! I can't help think about the princess. Lorali. How lucky she was to live in a place like this.

The sea snake coughs, interrupting my wondering, and nods her head upwards.

'Oh, sorry.' I scramble over to her, looking like a right nosy parker, but I can't help it, it's all so stunning. 'Pretty decent place to work!' I nudge the snake but she ignores me. Well that went down the hole like a rotten winkle.

Marcia Zs her body for me like a staircase, which is weird – I don't know how to use a staircase so I just float up as I normally would, using my hand to hold onto her jagged banister of a spine so she doesn't think I don't know how to be in a palace or something.

'Cheers.' I bow my head. Dunno what I do that for. Embarrassing.

The next floor is even greater, biggest I've ever seen, and so bright too. As if the genius sea designed every room with her hands. Small glowing sea-bugs and crazy neon fish light up corners. It's unreal invention. *And* there's a balcony and all.

But then I see the painting. A massive picture of her. Lorali. Like a photograph, her eyes leaping out of the wall, so deep and true to life. It's like a shrine now. Covered in flowers and more of those bug lights. It's proper beautiful. I am transfixed; imagining her living here, being in this room, sends chills up my spine.

The pattering of feet makes me jump. A sea-monkey in a butler suit hops towards me on two feet, interrupting my nosiness. His back is so straight – how do they train these creatures? He invites me to come closer before snootily opening up the door to reveal the most wonderful, bright room. The walls are made of smashed glass and glimmering stone – a mosaic of chipped crockery and rock.

And there he is. His Majesty. The king. In *real*, actual, life.

'Ahhh, there she is!' he greets me. He has a warm face with a long, dark beard, bushy brows and straight, dark hair. He is tanned and strong-looking but not as big as I'd imagined. Murray would say his tapestry was healthy and ripe; I'd reckon she'd say he was a good person with a gold heart – not that I'm any good at reading tapestries . . .

I bow to him. 'Your Majesty,' I offer.

'No, no, please do not bow to me. I hate all of that.'

'I'm sorry, Your Maj—'

'No. No. Stop all this fluffing and flapping and apologising – none of that.' He bats the air like he's trying to get rid of a bad smell, then he smiles. 'I like us to be equal.'

'Me too.' I smile back. That's a relief.

'We are *delighted* to welcome you to the palace and even more thrilled that you've taken on the position. It's quite a task.'

'I'm ready for a challenge.'

'I thought you might be, which is why your fellow Tips nominated you for the job, I'm sure. I've heard about your work, *Aura*— it is Aurabel, isn't it?'

'Yes, sir – Aurabel.'

'We know that you're politically engaged and very active; it's very impressive to see a young Tip like you be so ambitious.'

'To be honest, sir, I was surprised you'd even heard of me.' *Meaning, you've not visited Tippi once, EVER.*

'Ah, I have my sources.' He clasps his hands proudly. His crown is battered and perched awkwardly on the slant of his head, like it might slide off, like he hopes it might.

'We are so excited to invite you as the first participant of our new programme, where we are aiming for all Mer to work together – beginning with the rejuvenation of the much-loved forest.'

'I am excited too.'

'I, for one,' he says, as though he's rehearsed the words, 'am *so* looking forward to revisiting the forest once again and enjoying the tranquillity and charm the gardens have to offer.'

I nod. Trying not to laugh at the sweet little *king* speech he's prepared. 'Me too, Your Majesty.'

'I hope it gives you an enormous amount of pride to know that you have a hand in restoring it back to its original beauty.'

'It does! The other Tips are well jealous,' I joke cheekily. Zar considers me. He can't help it and begins to laugh. Breaking character.

'You are paving a way then!'

'Let's hope so.'

'Of course there will be a reward . . . a salary of sorts.'

TRY TO ACT NORMAL.

'But I think it best to wait until you've visited the forest to gauge how much work there is to be done before we talk business – but do not for a minute think we undervalue your work here in the Whirl. I can assure you that you will be rewarded handsomely for your bravery and creativity.'

I gulp. Nod. Think of Murray. Us both. Getting out of Tippi. *Going some place else, maybe?* I've got to try not to get ahead of myself.

'Sienna will meet you down at the forest. At the main entrance.'

I gape.

'I trust you know of Sienna?'

'Errrr . . . yeah,' I say, all dummy and star-struck. Course I know of Sienna. 'The keeper of beasts.'

'That's it.' He shakes his head. 'That Mer will be the death of me – oh, she keeps me in line, let me tell you, but I suppose you have to *be* a beast to keep one!'

I gulp. I am nervous to meet Sienna – I've heard so much about her. I feel my tapestry bleach pale, and the king comforts me. 'Don't worry, her bite isn't as big as her bark.'

We shake hands and I see him really looking at me, properly, right in the eyes, and something tells me that he is a good Mer. A good Mer who's gone through hell. I can't help but think of the painting of Lorali on the wall in the corridor. And as I turn to leave, the king says, 'I hope you have a fantastic day, Aurabel. Let this be the start of a wonderful adventure.'

I bow a bit and then remember he doesn't want me doing all that bowing business so I just do a small wave and leave the gorgeous room with the twinkling walls, happy as a toad in mud.

Then I see this head. Popping down from the floor above, hanging over the iron railings. A young Mer, about my age, who I've never seen before. His eyes nervously meet mine. I don't want to be rude or look inexperienced so I keep my head down and pretend to look like I know what I'm doing.

He swims down. He smiles at me. He has kind eyes and a soft face. He is what you would describe as 'handsome' though not my type, obviously – but I know Tips who would gobble him up. He has long hair that sweeps over his head to the side, a chiselled jaw, good nose, I'd say . . . if that counts for anything.

'I'm Kai,' he volunteers in a soft voice, as though it's a name that doesn't belong to him.

'Hi. I'm Aurabel.'

'Hello, Aurabel. That's a nice name.' His eyes light up.

'It's not,' I joke boldly. 'It's common as hell.'

'I've never heard of it before. I like it.' He smiles. 'Are you going to the forest?'

I nod.

His eyes widen. 'Are you going to open it up?'

'That's the plan.'

'Wish I could come with you.'

'Why can't you?'

'Not allowed.' I suddenly guess who he is. He's the king's salvaged.

'Don't worry,' I tell him. 'It's only because you're *royalty*. Once it's safe again you'll be able to go there all the time.'

'I don't even reckon I'll be allowed to go then.'

'Course you will. Once you're resolved you can do whatever you like!' Am I saying too much? I dunno how it is for these lot. I shouldn't be talking out of turn, especially not in the palace. 'Anyway, better get a wiggle on. Got work to do. Nice to meet you.'

'You too.'

He calls after me: 'Hey, maybe when you get back I can show you round the palace?' He looks kind of nervous as he says it. Maybe the poor sod doesn't have any friends.

'Yeah, defo.' And I swim away, letting the water take me.

The sea is warm and calm. The water is a salty lick of paradise, schools of fish springing in triangles, whales singing. I see a couple of faces from Tippers that I know. 'Awwwright!' I shout at them, all cocky. They look well jealous, like, *Where's she off to then?* Ha! Wouldn't *they* like to know? I thought I'd pretty much managed to tell the WORLD what I'm doing but obviously not. I pick up speed. I love swimming, my body all tight like a bullet, slicing through the sea. I am whipping through the water, light, feeling like the most precious thing in the world.

Lorali

GOLD

I don't tell Cheryl about the note. I want to but I don't. I don't want her getting her hopes up. I am scared to go alone too. I could take Flynn or Iris, but what if this is dangerous? I don't want to get anybody else hurt. I've done enough of that. Besides, the note wasn't meant for Iris or Flynn; it was meant for me.

I can't *not* go. What if it is Rory making contact? It would make perfect sense that he would want us to meet under the pier. Where we first met. But how had he shot the dart and not said anything to me? Shown his face? Reached out to me?

Cheryl pours more tea into my cup; watching the water rise I think about the petrified forest. Rory's words will be sunken now. Completely immersed. Framed like art on the walls. It has to be him who wrote the note. It has to be Rory. Does he still remember?

'Right then . . . blue or gold?' Cheryl rattles the nail polishes in my face, the yellow plastic washing-up bowl filled to the top with soapy hot water.

'Errrr . . . hands or feet?'

'Feet.'

'Gold.' I nod. 'Gold's a lucky colour.'

AURABEL

SIENNA

I pause outside the forest, too nervous to head in on my own. Course I want to; I miss the place like we all do. Not scared exactly – just don't want to do anything wrong, break any rules. It suddenly dawns on me that I'm about to meet Sienna. One on one. Spend the day with her, maybe. Sienna, the keeper of beasts and monsters. Absolute madness. I am buzzing. Sure, not everyone likes council member Sienna much. We all make up stories about how she is a proper evil witch – we spread all these rumours about how she'll eat you up. Still, that's kind of cool in itself, ain't it, really? Imagine *eating* somebody.

'Aurabel!' She arrives beside me in her serpent-pulled black chariot. The striped beasts hiss at me. 'Oh be quiet,' she mutters, but they hiss again. 'SILENCE!' she scorns. And they freeze. Jaws locked. They cower. Tremble in fear. Imagine making a beast *that* terrified of you! It's unreal.

Ducking from the oversized hood of her cape, she reveals herself. She is even more striking in real life. High cheekbones, creamy skin, silver eyelashes, powder-white brows. Her features are all pointy – even her teeth, which are fanged. Her nose is hooped with a bull ring at the centre. Her tapestry is complex, spinning my head with its illustrative make-up of code and texture – scaled like a reptile, dark and detailed. *Sienna, in the flesh*. Rah. Intimidated, star-struck, I grin, all toothy. Murray would *DIE* if she was here – Sienna is like a style icon. A true legend.

'Did you come here unattended?'

'Erm . . .'

'The king sent no guard to accompany you?'

I find myself double checking, like just in case he has and I haven't seen.

'Clearly not,' she mutters. 'That stupid king – he expects *you*, a Tip, to come out to the petrified forest and fend for yourself? Has he lost his mind? Does he know how *dangerous* that is?'

I feel sick. Yeah, why *didn't* he send me with guards? It didn't even cross my mind at the time.

'You went to the palace; why didn't he bring you here himself?'

I look down to the ground and shrug.

'Now that is just him all over. Typical. What a coward.' She snaps her gloves off. 'Move over and let a female get to it, already. He's in the wrong game!'

I'm not gonna lie: this is kind of pissing on my parade a bit. There I was feeling all chuffed and important and now I am feeling a bit like a skivvy. She raises her brows. 'Then again, you're just a waif to him, I suppose. He has no respect.' She digs the knife in. Is she right?

'I'm sure his heart is in the right place,' I stick up for him – he was nice back there. 'He knows I can protect myself.' But in the swelling of my gut I doubt my own words.

'You know the only reason he closed the forest was because he didn't want his salvaged to visit, in case he remembered anything,' she spits. 'It's so selfish.'

Kai. Of course. That makes sense. I start to feel angry. And small. Standing there in front of Sienna. I feel stupid for even believing a single thing that king said. All he did was go on and on about how unsafe the sea is. Am I that unimportant to the king that he'd just send me out on my own? Completely inexperienced? I mean, I know I am from Tippi but it doesn't mean I'm worth nothing. *Do your own errands in future then, you wimp!* I sniff hard. Don't want to humiliate myself even further in front of Sienna.

'Don't get upset; it's not your fault the petrified forest is dangerous. I'm sure it wasn't deliberate; he just wasn't thinking.' Sienna puts her hand out to me gently. 'It was *my* idea to employ you – this was *my* suggestion, *my* project – he probably thought I had it covered. Let's give the idiot the benefit of the doubt. It was probably a miscommunication.'

I nod. I knew it seemed too good an idea to have come from the king. This just makes me like Sienna even more.

'I shouldn't have had an outburst like that, not in front of you. You are going to have to get used to my temper if we are going to work together.' She smiles. 'It's just that sometimes I'd really like to, you know . . . strangle him!' We laugh together. I can see her point. I feel like only a good thing can come from us two being a team. Even if the whites of her knuckles are going on a bit strong like she actually does want to strangle him. Anyway . . .

I notice Sienna has a chain on her hand – a link. She spies me inspecting it.

'Ah, you're wondering about my chain. This connects me to my biggest beast, Nevermind, going all the way back to her cell. If she ever tries to escape, I'll feel her tug. She's terribly dangerous. It's imperative that I know where she is at all times.' She clears her throat. 'Besides . . . you never know when you might need a beast like her. This forest has been desolate for a whole year! Who knows what we'll find.'

We've all heard the stories about Nevermind. I shudder to think of seeing her in the flesh. Dawns on me how big and empty the sea truly is. I hope *she* doesn't get invited to the forest.

'Shall we?'

We swim into the forest. Curling around the spines of trunks, coiling the marigolds and pickerel weeds, dangling talons of beastly feathery sea quills and crusts of amber coral. Their brambles and thistles seem larger than usual and more chaotic. It wasn't that anybody tended to the overgrown shrubbery before, but it seemed to know our pathways, make space for our bodies to roam. Now it blocks us out, as though we are no longer welcome. Deeper and deeper we loop the labyrinth, combing our way through the knots of weed and ivy that have free rein. The only noise is the slurp of the water rippling about us from our own movements, and the licking sound of Sienna's serpents snaking behind us.

My own heartbeat.

Breathe. You're all right – you've got this . . . six, five, four . . .

'I've heard you're a very good hunter.' Sienna's voice is gravelly. Must be from all those years of talking to monsters – she now seems to have a voice like one.

'I eat well,' I joke, patting my belly. 'Actually, saying that, I hunt for so many of the Tips now, I'm usually the only one who goes without!'

'That's very sweet of you. Do you always do so much for others?'

'You've got to, haven't you? It's part of being alive. If I can help, then I do. Because you never know when you might need help yourself and hope there's someone knocking about to return the favour.'

'That's very true.' Sienna smiles and gently releases her serpents from their leash to graze and sniff about. I watch them snuffling out crabs and digging for fleshy prawns, listening to the clopping sound of their mouths working. I gulp. I've never been so close to this kind of monster before. I am in awe at how well she has them trained. Maybe something I could do in the future.

'You're a clever Mer . . . you want the best for your kind, don't you?' she asks me, her barbed fangs pressing into her painted lips. She speaks firmly. Formal but kind.

'Of course I do.' I nod. I am a bit addicted to looking at her face. She is so unique-looking. I kind of want a moment to just grab it and inspect it up close – have it all to myself without her judging me.

'Good – that's very good to hear.' She readjusts her position, claps her hands as if we're discussing business and then says in a very calm voice, 'I want you to know that I'm doing this for the greater good; it's not personal. I just cannot have this king in power any more. He isn't up to the job and he's driving our species into the ground.'

'OK . . .' I shake my head nervously. I mean, I have lots to say on the matter, I know all the Tips do – we aren't that happy with the way the kingdom is run. This could be my chance to have a voice.

'I think it would really make a stand if you were to not make it back to the palace today.' *What does she mean?* 'I think it would show just how unsafe the sea really is and, well, make that king look incompetent. Foolish. And that's what we want.'

I don't understand. Her words are chopping. Severe.

'There are monsters here. The sea isn't safe. He has put you in enormous danger. He is already despised. All it will take is one more little incident to really *tip* him over the edge. And he's done.' Our eyes lock. 'Making space for a real queen. Which is what we want. Isn't it?'

'I *guess*.' I sense danger. Can suddenly taste blood in my throat. But I'm trying to take her words in – she's important; I have to stay focused, listen to my instructions.

'By working with me, you will be memorable for ever. Making change. You will be a revolution.'

'Do you want me to work for you?' I ask, confused. 'Like, behind the king's back?'

'In a way, I suppose,' she lisps. Then her lip flickers. It's animalistic – can't explain it. Suddenly I just don't trust it. I feel unsafe. My instinct makes me do it. Something tells me to –

I launch backwards. Away from her. She laughs and slams

her hand on my shoulder. Knots her fingers around my hair. Snaps my neck back. *Got me.* Grabs me tight, her lips against my face, close to her. 'I am going to be queen and you are going to help me,' she growls.

'Help you how?' I am so scared I'm nearly sick. Trembling. I can barely breathe.

'Sometimes, Aurabel, one has to kill a cow to feed many mouths.'

I throw myself forward, darting fast. She drags me back by my hair and throws me to the forest floor. Dirt in my hands and mouth.

'Babies! Make it quick – she's a nice one. I'm sure she will be tasty too.'

No! No! Please! Don't! I beg and scream but I have to swim. Away. Fast. The serpents are coming for me, chasing me, *quick, quick, quick,* attacking, growling, biting, with gnashing teeth and claws and eyes that burn through me. And Sienna is sailing away, her back turned as I begin to taste my own blood.

Lorali

AT MIDNIGHT

I'm not a good sleeper. Cheryl knows that. She's slept like a baby since she came off the medication. She told me she sleeps better now than she ever did when Rory was around. Even though her missing boy is a drop in the depths of the sea, out of touch, still it gives her security, reassurance somehow. She never cries or wants him like somebody pining after somebody dead. She sleeps soundly, as if he is guarding her, protecting her always, squeezing into every hole in the wall; his love for her a blanket, with her all the time.

I think of her always when I lie awake at night. I lie where Rory did. Eyes at the blank ceiling, waiting for the fluorescent green stars to appear like on that first night. Lying in his bedroom. Slotting into his life like a foreign coin in an arcade machine. Waiting for hope to come in the form of a coma. *Where are you? What are you doing?* Breathing in the last of whatever scent was left of him in his bedroom, although it seems I have sniffed the life out of everything he touched. So now I just leave everything the way it is for him, allowing his mother to remind me of him every day.

I creep up. She's used to that. To the bathroom first to make things normal. I have an anxiety about bedwetting – there are new things to think about and some, especially at night, are out of my control. I flush the chain and in the wash of the water I bounce down the stairs and out into the summer night. Hastings is sleeping, lit only by the spilling amber of street lamps.

At the beach, I nervously grip onto my door keys in that knife-like position that Flynn taught me. *Aim for the eye. Aim for the eye.*

Over the stones I wobble and tip. There it is. The sea, with its unforgiving familiarity. The night so black and the water so cold. How could I have grown in this unforgiving mass of navy ocean?

The pier in sight, it all comes rushing back in a blur. When I first met him. When he found me.

I feel sick and squeamish from the butterflies. Excited. The thought of seeing Rory. My tummy whipping and flipping and jump-jacking in this trapping, cramping darkness. I feel selfish. I should have told the boys I was coming. Now I am small. I am a dot in the palm of nature. The big grand moon, staring, a Cyclops eye. *Shut up, you.*

Heart rattling in its cage, I step under the pier. The sea is moaning. A fat seal flops and rests in the water's break, which is a bit strange. But nothing else other than Hastings regulars: a few empty, browning crushed beer cans and burnt-out cigarette butts left over from summer. Pigeons coo. I check my phone.

I don't even know how to use the thing. But I'm on time. Chewing the soft fat on the inside of my mouth, I'm not sure whether to sit or stand. Not sure what my fate will be; who or what is wanting me if it isn't Rory – and if it is . . . *him* . . . do I look *OK*? Does he feel the same? I rearrange my pose – leaning, standing, hair folded behind my ear self-consciously. Why am I so nervous? Why am I so . . . And it's dark. Scary. Could be the journalists again . . . if it is, this is a nasty trick. To lure me here to ask questions – how am I feeling? *Still sad that your boyfriend drowned?* They'll never know the truth.

The seal leans up, its body gingerly thumping closer. Backing into the wall I hope whoever's coming comes quick. Still the seal, closer again, with her leathered rolls of blubbery fat, slamming down to the stones, dipping and rising, flippers sucking, glassy eyes fixed on me – and something makes me think that it might be the seal I have come here to see.

'Is it you?' Breathy almost-silent words tumble out from the ridiculousness of them. The seal stares back at me, with her big puddles of inky eyes. 'No . . . clearly not.' I shrug to myself, wrapping my arms around me.

The seal shakes her head. Flaps her flippers around her mouth. She rolls in the water, juddering, before recoiling, heaving up her body to standing. The seal then unpeels itself of her skin. Just like taking a coat off. No blood. No effort. Now a bundle of simple seal skin is on the floor and before me, standing, now I can take her in: the most striking, flawless, unclothed woman. Tall, statuesque; long, strong legs; elegant, slender arms and feminine, dainty fingers. Her hips and breasts are full and plump but not flabby like the coat of seal she

66

undressed from. A glossy, deep-chocolate stream of hair tumbles over her shoulder, her eyes, the same colour, staring me into a smudge.

'Lorali.' She is pleased to see me, like we have met before. *How does she know who I am?* Who is this? Was the seal a disguise? I can't be sure. 'Sorry to make you come out so late, but I couldn't risk showing you myself in the daylight. And I need you to take me seriously – you might not have believed me if I hadn't shown you who I was.' She speaks with little emotion, her sentences urgent but not rushed. Almost breezily flippant in her manner. I can't stop staring at the discarded skin next to her; how it slipped off her the way it did.

'Believed what?' I utter.

'That you and I have lots in common.'

'Do we?' I find that hard to believe, seeing her body.

'You are a fish who lives like a woman; I am a woman who lives like a fish.'

I am not a fish.

'Who are you? What do you know about me?'

'I am a Selkie.'

'A *Selkie*? The skin you came out of, was it seal? Are you half seal?'

'I'm not half seal nor half woman. Right now, as I am before you, I am whole woman. When I go back into the water I'll be whole seal. I'm never half of anything. Just like you, Lorali, I can move between two worlds.'

I shake my head. This isn't true.

'Lorali,' she says sharply, in a deep, serious tone. 'Rory is in danger.'

67

'Rory?' I stutter. I haven't heard his name in context for so long. Desperate for any news of anything about him I feel my heart shatter, urging to get to him. 'In danger how?'

'You must go down and save him.'

'Of course!' I panic. 'But how can I? I've surfaced, I'm a Walker now – I can't reverse. They told me. Once you surface you cannot return.'

'Yes, Lorali, they told you that because that is true. For *them*. NOT for you. Unlike me, you *are* half and you always will be half. Because you are different, because you were from a natural birth. You are unique.' She steps closer, her hands wrapping around mine now. She is boiling hot to the touch. She smells of the sea. Bitter. Tangy. Natural.

But she grips me harder, locks me into her stare, her eyes fierce. A warped groan comes from within her: a new voice, different from the controlled tone she had been speaking in just moments before. She is panicked, terrified. 'Do not listen to me, Lorali. Ignore and forget everything I say. Stay where you are. It's a lie.'

The naked woman bites her tongue, just as surprised as I am at the voice that came from her. I snap away from her grasp, snatching my hand out of hers. 'Who was that?'

'Who was what?' She regulates her composure, at war with the contradiction, ignoring her split personality.

'How is Rory in danger?' My patience, from fear, has gone. Tears welling but I suck them back. I don't want her playing on my vulnerability. 'Tell me right now, or I'm leaving.'

'The sea is not a safe place, little Lorali. But you can rescue him, before his resolution. You can bring him back to land.'

68

'How can I trust you?'

'You CAN'T!' the deeper, more desperate voice roars before being once again trapped within.

'I have no reason to lie to you, Lorali.' She smiles sweetly and it seems so genuine this time. Any word of Rory seems to weasel its way to my heart and melt me down.

The sound of seal cry beckons from the water behind her. 'I have to go. Don't think on it for too long; his resolution is sooner than you think.' A baby seal's head pops up from the water, then another. The woman smiles at them and reaches for her seal skin as though she's picking up her coat at the end of a party, and confidently walks towards the water.

'Wait!' I call out. 'Who salvaged him?'

But the woman is already once again seal, and gone.

THE SEA

BLOODY PEARL

Finally, when all is quiet, the lid of the shell opens. The hinges of the jaw of it yawn apart, the opaque enamel scuffed and chipped. Covered in the scratches of their claws. But now, as water, I am still. I am everywhere. Sifting, calm and endless.

The coast, clear. Her hands, bloody, covered in the stuff, dragging wrists and elbows. Her long, blue hair riddling out of the shell's mouth like a complicated love song. Her eyes, rapid still. *Have they gone? How long has it been?* Hobbling out of the shell, she grinds forward. *Why can't she move her tail? Where is she?* Clambering out, she grips the lipped edge of the shell to steady herself, thanking it for being there when she needed to hide from teeth.

Whispers; red plumes of bloody smoke. Swirling in my heart. She is blinded by her own blood. The red mist of the Whirl fogs her vision. All she can hear is a fizzy, high-pitched, unnatural shrill blocking both her ears. A tinnitus cry seems to be coming from within. Her adrenaline makes her tremble. Her tapestry is bleeding. More than that – it is broken. She is sure of it. It will need stitching, urgently.

She has to get back. The palace isn't far . . . *Or is it?* She doesn't even know where she is. She tries to swim, to snake her hips and wave her fin, but the weight is too much. It isn't painful but that is what worries her: that she can't feel the pain. The fear, yes. The needling sting of shock too. And relief. Relief that she is still breathing. Still here. That is something; means she isn't dead altogether.

But where is the pain? Pain means that she is *alive*. Nerves aren't responding.

She goes into a methodical trance of staying alive. Survival. She is losing a lot of blood. Her colours are fading; she still can't see from all the blood. She speaks to herself calmly. 'You're OK,' she says. 'You're OK.'

Not me, though. I say nothing.

She is already beginning to sink and so she allows herself to sink to the bottom. There she can see to her wounds. Her tail. It has to be broken. *Let's take a look . . .*

Down.

Down.

Down.

The way she was recognised: her long teal hair. She has been told it is 'hair more beautiful than the sea itself'. Now, tangled with the red of blood, it looks like theatre. Her arms span like kites, sailing her downwards. A flying big-top circus tent, twirling towards the grit. Her eyes closed. The moment of hope before she faces the mirror of her tapestry. It would tell all in the reflection. Develop like a Polaroid. *Hold onto that*

71

moment. My guts bleed for this Mer, for what she is about to find when she sits on the seabed, on the sand with the snaps of crescent-moon shells, down on the level of the hermit crabs and claws that scuttle and scamper on my ocean floor. When she opens her eyes and screams. Because she will realise that she was wrong: her tapestry, just like her blood pearl necklace, is not broken at all.

It is gone.

AURABEL

HEART ON THE EARTH

It's the pain that wakes me. So I wasn't dead then. But the only thing alive inside of me is the memory that I relive.

First the ripping of flesh. The panic. The bigness of it all and swallowing. So quick. The noises coming from me drowned out in the hugeness, silencing my attack. Rough as hell. Tearing flesh. Breaking bones. The hazy muffled screams and licks of fanged tooth in skin – and then piercing. Roaring. Tearing. Screaming. Crying. *Don't.*

I saw the shell. My rescue. An oversized trapdoor. I remember how it wouldn't lift, wouldn't come apart, but I could see it was empty. Damn thing wouldn't open, jammed together with all this white crust. Fingers breaking on the rough surface, knuckles bleeding and still screaming – suddenly it let me in. I managed to shut the thing down just before they finished me off. They roared and scratched at the shell until they decided I was done.

Then it was after. When I saw. Really drank it all in. The reality. When the world had slowed. That jagged edge taken off.

Lost its bite. *Clawing. Ripping. Clenching. Grabbing.* Grabbing *anything*. Muscle. Bone. Arms. Wrists. Grit. Veins. *Argh*. Loose. Apart. The sand. Weaving. Slushing. Not enough. Raking hands. No grip. Too weak. A stone. A dead, cold stone. That was me. Useless. A corpse. A dead, useless, fucking stupid stone. Heart on the earth. Sliding. A cripple. A joke. Fuck it. NO. FUCK IT. Paralysed. FUCK. Paralysed as fuck. FUCK.

Fuck you, Sienna. FUCK. I'll kill you, bitch. She set those beasts on me. To her I was some nobody Tip. Well, fuck her. She couldn't even watch them get me. Coward. Fuck that council. FUCK HER. Fuck that weak king. *Soggy twat*. Shove your job up your –

FUCK.

The pain was blinding. Still. Course I had to save my brain. Couldn't do any of that nutty nut-bag business where you start overthinking for *what if*'s sake. Can't rewind time now. I roll over in the cruddy ground. I must have slept here. Dunno how long it's been. Don't even know how I'm meant to start again. Can't go back to Tippi. Not like this. Those beastie Tips will eat me up for breakfast once they learn that I'm only half a Mer now. That I'm half the Mer I was. I'll be bottom of the pack. I might even lose Murray. Wait – my pearl! My pearl. My neck is bare. Where's it gone?

DON'T CRY, AURABEL.

Murray. My heart's bleeding, I swear.

Six, five, four, three . . .

Six, five . . .

74

THE SEA

A PLACE FOR DREAMING

Aurabel rises from her half-grave of sea earth and salt ruins and looks up to see that she is not in the place she had been but somewhere completely different. Still, too much too soon.

First, with her last remaining strength, she winds as much palm leaf around her wound as she can find. Working quickly against the irresistible gnawing beg of fatigue, she bandages herself, emotionless. If for one moment she thinks about her tragedy she will go under. Numb with pain, she imagines her disaster belonging to somebody else. A stranger. She is helping *them*. *Yes*. 'Don't worry,' she even mumbles with encouragement. 'You're all right. I'm sure it won't scar bad.'

Mummified up, heaving the weight of her upper self, she bravely heads into the first shelter she finds. A small cave; even though it is dark; even if it is home to a monster, it will be a small monster. Monsters have half of her anyway, she decides; lucky them if they manage to make that half a whole.

Lorali

TWO MINDS

In the bath. I soak.

Cloudy silence. *Drum. Drrrrruuuum.* Beating against my ears like the electronic radio. The pumping thump of new blood gushing, running, feeding through my veins and shooting messages to my brain. *Tell me what to do.* Out again and under, take a breath. Drown again in soapy suds of lavender and vanilla. Little globes of rainbow-froth bubbles trace my skin. Wash myself off. This warming, imposing loneliness could kill me if I let it. The Selkie. *What does she know? Does she know more? Does it mean I have to go back? Why did she contradict herself? Why did I feel the seal was saying something different than the woman inside her?* And Rory . . . could he really be in danger?

Is it better to smash up my new life myself with control or ignore it and wait for the cracks to tear it apart anyway? These borrowed legs I have could even fool me. Yes, *real,* but I have sacrificed for them. Selfish. Here I play house in this pretend domesticated storyline that isn't mine to tell. Pull the plug; don't think too much. Let the worry spill away.

I am a teenage girl in a bath. A teenage girl who likes the smell of shampoo. I like chicken nuggets and listening to music. I have learnt how to read. How to bake a cake. I walk weirdly. I trip up nineteen times a day. I like cake and tea and crumpets. I am not good with spicy food. I have a mole by my belly button that looks like a cookie crumb. I really love dogs. I like the cinema. I like getting a bit drunk. I like the theatre. I cry my eyes out when people clap in large rooms. I like watching babies in prams. I like watching old ladies catch up on the benches in the park and when strangers give homeless people half of their sandwich. I have legs and feet.

I'm not doing anything wrong. I'm just trying to carry on.

Though the shadows and marks on the tiles in the mottled marble of the bathroom walls sometimes make the expressions of worried women's faces. Their bony, crooked, pleading mouths, their frowning heads and sad eyes, they fill me with guilt. With dread. *What are they telling me to do? Where are they wanting me to go?*

Rory. A warm tear treads carefully down my face. Because I am scared. Because I miss him. I am too weak.

'Lorali, love, fancy a glass of wine?' Cheryl calls from the hallway. I wipe my face, rub my eyes, sit up urgently, the foam slithering down my spine. I grip onto the edges of the bath.

'Ooh yeah, lovely,' I shout back. 'Be out in a minute.' With a wet hand I reach for the towel on the floor next to me, leaving a splatter of dirty bath water on the tiles below.

THE SEA

ADVENTURE

And when she wakes she screams at the wrapped blood-blotted stump attached to her, replacing what had been hers. Allowing her raw, rasping hellish shrieks to rip and ricochet off the roof of the cave. Her bloody fists punching the hard grey slate beneath her and bawling and howling until her knuckles show white bone. So heavy is her heart I am surprised she does not fall through the floor of the cave itself with the tugging weight of it. Hugging her bottom half close and then just as quickly rejecting it. Tough to watch. But she is tougher. As the musicality of that small, still, strong voice inside her whimpers. Aurabel stops crying. And then, in the new morning brightness, she sees it. Where she is.

In the blundering emptiness it appears out of nowhere. The colossal metal jagged machine world towers over her. A sunken, once steam-fuelled theme park that still speaks of *dreams*. Of turning spiked wheels; scribbles of winding tracks that seem to spiral; tall, upside-down uneven spindly bridges made of odd ends of fallen pieces of discarded mechanical leftovers; car parts, engines, factory works, carts, buggies, cranks, tools. Iron. Steel. Silver. Tin. She crawls, like the ghost of a pregnant spider, through the derelict land of industrial architecture until nature shows its face and gives her comfort.

Aurabel marvels at the way creatures gobble up the mammoth iron legs of the structures. Ivy and small fish have made homes on the arms of bridges. Barnacles stubbornly kiss the cluttered buildings of the fallen fairground. Candy-striped tents, cracked blushing Punch and Judy puppets still angrily tangled in mid-attack. Stuffed machines are now stocked tanks, home to fishes instead of teddy bears and toys. Rubber ducks, prizes, games behave as foreign plants with stems made from the snag of strangled let-down balloons, their colours faded too soon. Some innocent hell of a ghost train, the scares worn, is now a cosy comfort for a dozing starfish. Rusted dodgem cars, paint bubbling on metal like acne and the deceased bulbs marking the graves of immortal Walkers. Somehow, I found a stillness in this adventure land, a peace in this place to repair. Its whale song is spangled, a frenzied flurry laced with the haunt of family laughter and screams of dizzy bliss and dumpy clown-clumsy upside-down paradise noises. Now frozen, like some ageing haunted remains, capturing the leftovers of a once-forever party. The blend of past and present.

Of nature and machine.

As the night begins to bleed into my blue, I become blacker and colder, empty and hard. She can't. At all. Not in the terrible limbs of this stalking nowhere. Her head to the ground, she sinks, her open mouth in the earth . . . and then dazzle. Hundreds of lights coming from the small glow-bugs clinging to the fallen land; they shine. Just for Aurabel, just to guide her in this struggle.

Why does it feel like this fairground has tipped off the edge of the pier just for her? She has found a flicker of hope that perhaps she can fix this . . . It's not as if she is exactly short of tools . . .

And at the foot of the heap of abandoned junk offering out a screwdriver, a spanner, a bolt. Promising it has more to give, the metal mountain opens to her; plenty more where that came from. Burrowing deep, Aurabel begins to weed out objects that will do.

Up on her throbbing stump, Aurabel whispers to herself in reassurance as she raids the scrapheap. Carefully averting her eyes away from the reflection of herself in the wall of silly mirrors where everything seems a joke; a joke so funny, she almost laughs.

AURABEL

AMUSEMENT

Is this adventure laughing in my face?

The screaming of Walker girls and boys who I will never know.

Buried souls, for ever in the simplicity of being turned upside down, around and around.

Applaud.

This freak cannot laugh any more.

When it was built, the Walker who made it, did she or he ever think this happy-making paradise would be the grave to a Mer?

Did they ever imagine that I would lose myself inside its ugly tease of a jungle? Its torturing swirls that hallucinate and so . . .

Trippy you could climb the walls with the tip of your nose.

I thought I knew Walkers but this has thrown me, this horror land of fantasy; I cannot place it – or its purpose – this . . .

Dummy-dodo.

Horror show.

Strange Walkers with painted faces and frilly necks and fluffy balls lined down their chest and spooks and shadows.

And pointed arrows.

Eyes in every cranny and crook.

And shapes that overlap and play and torment and fuse these brave colours.

And pumps and wires.

And stuffed animal guts.

Jack-in-the-box, square bluntness, repeat.

HA HA HA.

Everybody looks happy but their smile is so forced.

On the walls of this dreamland set-up.

A curiosity that maybe I can understand . . .

Maybe I can find solace in this fallen amusement? This terrible joke. This comedy of errors. Is there sanctuary for me in the burial of this monster den?

Have I landed in hell or made a friend?

THE SEA

OOPS . . . ONE MOMENT

Before we return to land I just want to stop in on Sienna. See if guilt has anything to say.

Sienna is there, yes, but guilt, sadly, is nowhere to be seen. The king has sent many messengers but Sienna has not responded; let him sweat it out before he hears the news himself. The serpents take turns to vomit up the pieces of raggy tail, sections of a mangled puzzle that together make up Aurabel's tapestry. Evidence that the deed is done is rewarded with treats and cuddles in the parlour.

She will sleep soundly tonight, no doubt, knowing her precious monsters had their bellyful, in the form of a little harmless Mer from the poor, wet town of Tippi.

But what she does not know is that they only got the half of her and will go to bed hungry.

THE SEA

TANKED FISH

Opal Zeal now calls the Royal Penthouse suite at the five-star luxury hotel The Dorothy, in London, *home*. Mainly for the golden bathroom, the deep-lipped tub and the penthouse view of the River Thames. London: a blurry spill of soggy ink coughing into a wet newspaper. But it is the spa in the basement of the hotel itself that has become useful to Opal. A hiding place to exist on a diet of room service. A den in which to crumble, to cringe, to confide, to celebrate.

In this clear-watered, naturally salted pool (when they say 'naturally' they mean thanks to me, of course they do) just for her, complete with frothy massage jets, Opal whiles away the days. It even has a vibrating bench that she can sprawl across whilst she has her meetings. But not everybody is quite so keen on the waterworks. What was once a novelty for the hotel is now becoming tiresome. At first the accommodating staff were more than happy to laminate any paperwork Opal had to oversee, but she can tell some of the younger Walkers are getting slightly fed up of her constant demands. The way she sits here today like always. She is a mermaid. And *STILL* a celebrity.

Marco, her shiny publicist, is also tiring of the makeshift 'office' spa attire, having sported every eccentrically revealing designer Speedo imaginable. Maintaining the ginger-biscuit spray tan and Abs Attack classes whilst taking care of Opal and her demands isn't always a doddle. He hasn't factored in the time for her *depression*. 'Emo' doesn't look *great* on the schedule. Marco prefers the fruitful highs of their relationship: slurping expensive cocktails on luxurious roof terraces, designer gifting days, high tea at Claridge's, eggs benedict at The Wolseley, pistachio ice cream at Fortnum & Mason, front row at the fashion shows, screenings, red carpets, parties at the Serpentine. Yes, the highs are great but the lows are dismal.

Opal's false nails are being aggressively filed, furiously, beside her. She slurps coconut water that has never touched a coconut. Her curves hug her bikini top – designer, of course – creamy, juicy butterscotch flesh squeezing out, a plunging cleavage couching her solid-gold name necklace: ZEAL, written in italics. That way she can *always* spell her name when it comes to signing contracts – just hold the pen straight and follow the letters.

'Take my hair out, would you?' Opal scratches at her scalp with her free hand. 'Can't stand this stupid wig. They bake it, you know? In an *oven*. To set it.' Another therapist nods and begins to unpeel Opal's hair, pins and clips, unleashing the smell of muted hairspray. 'Ouch! Be careful!' she spits, angrily reaching inside her jewelled bikini top and fishing for a little pill. Opal pops the warm-upper, washing it down with a tepid glug of 'coconut'.

'I'm fat, aren't I?' Opal prods her belly. 'I've put on weight.'

'Darling, never!' Marco lies, but this *is* something he's been intending to bring up with her – now just isn't the time.

'It's fine, you don't need to lie; I'm getting there. You can tell me. It's not my fault. It's the food here. Ugh. It's all those Krispy Kreme donuts, cheeseburgers, brownies . . . the chocolate milk – what evil person *even* invents something so good?'

The *click-clack* of high-heeled shoes rattles over the slate tiles. It's the receptionist with her stiff jaw and slick hair and triangle red lips.

'You have guests.'

Opal looks disappointed. She just wants to get drunk and relax, not have a meeting. Still, she has a plan up her sleeve, as always, to make the meeting a little more . . . fun.

Two Japanese chefs. Let's call them Chef A and Chef B to avoid confusion. Both Chef A and B politely refused the suggestion of wearing bathing suits to the meeting and attempt to shuffle in, propping themselves at the edge of the pool on chairs. Ugly blue carrier bags over their shiny black leather shoes for 'hygiene reasons'. Hands awkwardly splayed on kneecaps like smooching starfish.

'Why not roll your trousers up? Dip your feet in?' Opal pushes.

'Thank you, Miss Zeal; we are more than happy as we are.' Chef A bows his head. 'Did you get the sample menus?'

'Oh yes. Lots of them are new to me but I trust your taste. I can't wait to try the dishes.'

'It is very funny for us, Miss Zeal,' Chef B dares to joke. 'We never thought a mermaid would choose to serve sushi.'

'What can I say? I'm a cannibal bitch.' Her face gives in to a sarcastic sideways smile the shape of a leaf. 'You could argue that one would never think a human would eat a pig . . . but here you are, eating it.'

Marco tips his head back, snorting boyishly. The gentlemen politely laugh and the sake arrives. Just to make things a little more awkward.

'A-MAZE-BALLS!' Marco shrills and greedily snatches the bottle from the waitress's tray. Opal blushes; she feels the eyes of the chefs on her. *Are they judging me?* she asks herself. Marco fills the glasses. 'Gents?'

The chefs refuse. Chef A addresses the matter head on, as he is Chef A after all. 'It is too early for us to drink, but thank you. Please go ahead.'

Opal tries not to take their refusal personally. The nail therapist shifts her gaze to me, the water.

'What a bore! Suit yourself. More for us!' Marco turns to Opal. 'To you, Opal, and your stunning restaurant, Zeal.'

'To Zeal – thank you, Marco.'

Marco and Opal chink glasses and Marco proceeds to down the glass of sake like a shot of sambuca. The two chefs try to keep straight faces. Chef B considers nudging Chef A in the ribs but decides against it.

'Bleugh!' he winces. 'It ain't no pina colada, is it?' He coughs in the faces of the chefs.

'It's an acquired taste,' Chef B offers, proudly.

'Hmm. For those that like horse piss. Anyway, cheers.'

'Congratulations,' Chef A smiles, 'but there is a lot of work to do before we can relax. And then still no time to relax!' He chuckles. 'Owning a restaurant is just about the most stressful job on the earth.'

'This is the calm before the thunderstorm!' Chef B chips in.

'Let's press on then.' Opal takes out a piece of chewed-up bright-pink bubblegum from her mouth and sticks it to the poolside. 'Would you mind coming in? You sitting there is making me feel awfully uncomfortable. I just can't be myself.'

'I am sorry, we didn't bring our bathing suits. We have a long day of meetings ahead of us.'

Opal smacks her lips together, unimpressed. Her eyebrow arched, she glances down at her nails.

'You want us to get into the water –' Chef A shakes his head – 'naked?'

'Nobody said naked,' Opal says.

The chefs glance at each other and then at Marco. But he isn't interested – he is on Opal's verified Twitter account tweeting to her sixty-five million followers the word 'ZEAL' followed by a prayer emoji. *How mysterious.*

And so the men step down into the Jacuzzi bath, fully dressed in their suits, as Opal's claws become hot pink.

'We have the plans here; photographs of how the building work is coming along.' Chef A glances at his papers only to see them soaking up a puddle of water on the side of the pool, spoiled into an inky blur. 'However it seems you'll have to come and see it in person.'

'Oh yes –' Opal bats them away, almost disinterested – 'I have a glass bath on wheels, so I can come in that, no problem,' Opal reassures them. 'And we are still having the black cod?'

'Yes, Miss Opal Zeal.'

'And the cocktails?'

'Yes, of course, Miss Zeal.'

The receptionist trip traps in again: *click, clack, click, clack* . . .

'Your guests have arrived, Miss Zeal.'

Three more chefs enter, also Japanese. Let's name them Chefs C, D and E, for clarity. Chefs C, D and E are all very surprised to see chefs A and B in the pool. They know of each other's work, this is clear – they are all owners of competitive Michelin-starred restaurants. It gives the new arrivals great pleasure to see their rivals fully clothed in a Jacuzzi with a mermaid and an imp. Until Opal wipes the grins off their faces.

'Get in,' Opal orders.

'But we –'

'Do you want the job?'

'Forgive me, Miss Zeal, but I thought it was us designing the menu for Zeal?' says the already soaking Chef B.

'Your ignorance is *forgiven*.' She gives a rough, forced grin. 'You are designing a menu for Zeal. I didn't say I would choose it.'

'You cannot do this. We have a contract.' Chef A argues.

'I can do whatever the hell I like. I'm a mermaid. Who is going to tell me anything?'

'She has a point,' Chef D admits and gets down into the water. Chefs C and E follow; E is murmuring in Japanese under his breath; both are taking their phones and wallets out of their pockets, their watches off.

'In a moment –' Opal sinks another sake – 'I'm going to release a sea bass into the water.' The chefs look stunned, confused, pissed off. 'The first to catch it, kill it and turn it into sushi before my eyes will become head chef.'

'This is going to be brilliant.' Marco sits back, giggling. 'Opal, you're crazy!'

'This is a joke. You can't humiliate us like this,' Chef C argues. 'I won't do it.'

'Don't do it then, your choice, but you will *not* be working at Zeal.'

'I've worked hard on that menu!' Chef E frowns.

'I haven't even brought along my knife,' Chef C says in Japanese but don't worry, I've taken the time to translate it for you.

On cue, Opal's security enter, each carrying a sharpened Yoshihiro Shiroko Kasumi knife, and begin handing the knives to the seated, soaking-wet chefs. Next, a fish, tanked, is set on the side next to Opal. The fish is springing about, darting about in a panicked rush. Gluey, grey eyes teary and pressed. Its skin silver, electric. The chefs murmur to each other. Take the knives. One loosens his tie; another cricks his neck. Eyes focused. *What if they cut Opal by accident?* Now *that* would be funny.

It is hot in the sauna; pearls of sweat begin to trickle down the chefs' foreheads.

'What are the rules?'

'Just as I said: first to make sushi is head chef. Simple as that.'

The men nod. Opal turns her half-manicured nails to the clasp of the tank, ready to submit the vulnerable sea bass to the thrashing knives.

But what is the *click-clack* of the receptionist doing here again now? Her twisted lip-glossed mouth clenches. 'Miss Zeal, your guest has arrived.'

Not more *chefs*, surely?

Or better yet . . . a shark?

'Who now? We aren't expecting anyone.' Marco shrugs.

And through the licking flames of fire she appears. In an oversized rib-knit jumper, faded denim blue jeans and worn, tired pumps, it is her.

Lorali.

Opal freezes. Her heart in her throat. She speaks calmly, her eyes not moving from Lorali's for even a second to blink. Lorali does not say a word.

Opal gestures with her hands for privacy. 'Gentleman, you may leave. I'll have Marco be in touch once we have revised the menus.'

'But what about the fish?'

'I've changed my mind. Release that fish back into the sea. Now.'

AURABEL

TAPESTRY

With bloody fingers.
   Rifling, mending, mixing.
   Feels wrong.
   Transforming.
   Like borrowing a set of wings.
   I could use the metal to bash my brains out . . .
   Nah. That's the easy route.
   Come on you – you're all right.
   I stitch up the new scales.
   Shaking, this needs a dainty hand.
   Not mine.
   To assemble, threading, blood slice, thin line of red streak.
   And curdling.
   Wound salt is a bitter mix of wincing and messy work.
   What with the blood and grit and sand.
   But it feels that the water is somehow on my side and keeps
as still as she can be to help me.

Let the speed slow. I am an empty cup. Dizzy and faint and clumsy and missing the point.

Lost my bite.

Sewing up the old stump first and keeping the right bits in that need to be left in.

Like the stomach, of course, and the liver, the heart, the lungs . . .

I shake my head. I'm mad. Fear is here, of course – *Oh hi, fear*. But not just that – it's all laughable. No. Not now. Gentle work. Quick, quick.

Shake. Again. Nearly fade away. Need food. All these sugary packets on the floor of this stolen place but I can't tell what's safe to eat.

Dig for sap.

Mud in nails and scab.

Eat sap.

Better already.

Rushing. Blood.

Under the lights.

The sky beating bold blue. Black. White. The stir of clouds mottles the surface and paints pictures on the roof of the sea.

If I'm going to make my own tail, I'm going to make it the best tail ever, with gadgets of snatches and wheels and hooks *with* speed.

An industrial hulk of metal.

Of odd ends and findings, its make-up, a clockwork skeleton of machinery bones.

Slithers of rusted baked-bean tins replace scales and springs and soft coils behave as muscle.

Even if I die doing it.

Least I'll kill the time until I do.

THE SEA

MURRAY

It was like she knew.

When she didn't feel her arms around her waist, didn't hear her annoying humming first thing and woke to find no eel by her bed. She knew that something was wrong. And it felt like all the eyes of Tippi were on her that morning . . . the morning that Aurabel never came home.

Why didn't she come home?

It was like she had woken up on the wrong side of the earth.

She left Aurabel's slam without even trying to tie up her hair, her make-up still caked around her eyes and her heart mashing in her chest.

'Murray?' Titi shouted after her. 'Murray, what's wrong?'

But she ignored the voices of her Tips as she rushed past the morning bustle, desperate to know more, annoyed at herself for falling asleep; she'd wanted to know how her day had gone. But now she was numb, out of her body, heading for the Whirl . . .

* * *

Imprisoned within the perimeter of the palace walls, outside there is nothing Kai can do, nowhere he can venture, nobody he can talk to without the fretful eye of his father, Zar, hawking. Yes, he has a luxurious grand room of his own with instruments and games, the best food, the *best* protection . . . but as he peers his head over the gates or wanders down from his room, it does make him feel glum and envious to see the other Mer flipping and swimming about whilst he is kept to the gardens. He has no friends, no company . . . he doesn't want to do anything dangerous . . . he just wants to live.

Not long now though, boy, Zar reassured him. *After you resolve you can be as free as the ocean itself*. But the likeliness of that promise ever realising seems to dull by the day.

It is harder now. Mer often cling in clusters around the gates in protest. Zar told his boy to ignore them as he plays in the garden but it isn't always easy for Kai to not retaliate when these Mer make scathing comments about his father. Easier said than done to switch his ears off from the rebelling and rioting. Locked up, upstairs in his tidy little bubble, where everything is all right. It will be better once the forest is open. They will have somewhere to vent. Maybe he can even convince his father to let him venture there too?

Today Kai plays with the seal-pups, supervised under the watchful eye of the palace guard, the sea snake Marcia. But then he sees her.

Her hair is long, falling in swirls around her back. She has helpless purple eyes. *Pretty, yeah*, Kai decides. Marcia is resting her head on the seagrass – he could just go over whilst she sleeps.

'May we help you?' Kai asks her nervously in that same way he has heard Zar speak to Mer in the past. Using the 'we'. His voice getting lost in the braids of vines wrapping the railings.

'Excuse me.' Murray, a novice herself in these situations, utters in her most formal and responsible tone, in the same way *she* has watched other Mer approach the gates of the palace. 'May I please . . . err . . . speak with His *Majesty Sir Royal Highness please, the king?*'

Kai can't help but crack a smile. He clenches the pups' ball in his hands, the pups snuffling around his tail, waiting excitedly for him to throw it once again.

'Do I just talk to you? Or . . .' Murray nervously fills the silence, her hands gripping around the bars like a prison cell.

Kai is learning quickly about the hierarchy amongst Mer. How is he seen as superior to those outside the palace gates? He'll never know. He's never known any different. The pups begin to yap impatiently, hurtling themselves off each other and panting.

'All right, all right.' Kai laughs at them and sends the ball shooting through my waters. 'Go get it!' he babbles playfully as the ball springs out of sight, and the pups frantically scurry after it.

The hurry opens a snoozing eye from Marcia, her job being to guard and protect the palace and Kai, *not* sleep. She spins out of a spasm dreamily before attentively darting over to Kai.

Murray mutters nervously as Marcia investigates her. Marcia growls.

'Maybe if you could just tell the king that I need to speak with him?' Murray retracts. Marcia grunts. 'I shouldn't have come.'

'It's OK, Marcia.' *It is just a girl from Tippi*, Kai guesses. *What harm can she do?* Marcia screw-faces the Tip. 'Marcia, *that* is a *dirty* look. Very rude.' Kai strokes Marcia's chin. 'Don't mind her – go on . . .'

Murray softens and is able to speak.

'It's just my mate – she came to work for you yesterday –'

'Yeah, with the blue hair? Aurabel, is it?'

'Yes, Aurabel. That's her.' Murray's eyes light up. '*Yes!* Well see, she never came home, like she never returned from work – I mean, I knew she might be kept late here but I just wanted to make sure –'

'No, she never came back to the palace either.'

'She didn't?' Murray frowns. 'Did she come back from the forest?'

Murray is like nothing Kai has seen before. His reset soul stutters; he doesn't want to let her down but he doesn't want to lie. But it wouldn't look good. Not on his father, to lose a Mer on his watch. He has given the Mer a chance. It wasn't advised. She was inexperienced. A Tip too. It would backfire. Already he was hated. But if this gets out the Whirl will seem unsafe. *Savage.* He'll have put her at risk. Of course he can't say that, not to this terrified, pretty Mer at the gates. Shame the young boy's tapestry isn't resolved yet so she can't read if he is even telling the truth or not. I can tell you that he is.

'I wouldn't worry. It's safe in the Whirl. I really wouldn't.' Kai doesn't know if this is true or not as the Whirl is something so removed from him that it is intangible. He lives inside it, but he does not *know* it, nor what it is capable of. 'But I can ask for some searchers to go look for Aurabel to put your mind at rest,' Kai suggests, eager for the mission, to *do* something with himself. Meanwhile, Marcia marks his every move vigilantly.

'Kai!' It is the king. Murray has never seen him this close before. His long dark beard and angry bushy brows. His voice startles her. 'Come inside now, boy!'

'But, Father, I'm just speaking –' Kai explains, trying to argue. 'It's about the Mer, Aurabel, who came to work for us yesterday and never –'

'Inside. NOW!'

'You were worried for her too yesterday; you were –'

'NOW!'

Kai mouths, 'Sorry,' to Murray before gloomily turning away and heading back inside the palace. Murray sighs deeply. The palace gates have never seemed so tall. The Whirl has never seemed so big. And without the king helping, she will just have to find Aurabel herself.

And on her way back into Tippi she feels the change in currents before she sees the crowd. *Whose chariot is that parked by the fallen plane?* The square is lit with the hollowed eyes of her town and they part when Murray enters, making an aisle for her to swim up. Tapestries are grey and purple. Cracked and dull. No one will look at her now. She shakes her head in confusion, her own one blushing now – *What is going on?*

'Murray . . .' Orina's voice breaks the silence. 'We have a visitor.'

Nobody ever visits Tippi. But there she is, in the flesh: Sienna. Council member, beast keeper . . . here in Tippi, and she speaks.

Death, herself, has something to say.

'I'm afraid I have some bad news . . .'

98

Murray remains strong. Upright. Listening. Although she feels like a jellyfish, boneless, and wants to collapse, she doesn't. Her colours shrink out of her like a tie-dye run clean, her organs scooped out, like the middle of her could fall through.

'How?' Murray poses the question like an arrow.

Sienna catches the blade with her fingertips and answers, cool: 'The petrified forest is an overgrown forest, full with monsters.'

Murray swallows hard as the truth cuts and the Tips gasp.

'You were meant to protect her!' Titi, another Tip, snarls. 'They are *your* beasts.'

'It happened before I arrived onto the site,' Sienna lies. 'Aurabel was sent to the forest by the king to meet me; we got there too late.' Sienna bows her head and then lifts it when she feels the timing is right. 'A savage monster got to her before we could.'

Murray wants to tell them all that Aurabel was a very good hunter, that she was strong and smart. But her mouth can't make the shape of words. She is frozen.

'Why wasn't the king there? Why wasn't anybody protecting her?' Orina demands. 'I thought the whole point of this was to join forces. We were told she would be protected.'

'This is why I've come to Tippi,' Sienna begins. 'To apologise. Of course I feel utterly responsible for this.'

'So you should!' a gutsy Tip shouts.

'What good is a sorry now?' Titi snaps back and the others all join in, cursing and shouting.

'It's not your fault,' Murray mumbles to Sienna. The Mer quieten as Murray begins to talk. 'At least you've bothered to come. Aurabel hated that the council never made the effort to visit Tippi. I've just been to the palace myself and the king wouldn't even see me. Now I know why. He is guilty. He is a coward.'

'Yes, he is,' Sienna says. 'I see that now. But, Murray, this is about to change. We are going to make sure nothing like this ever happens again.'

'How?'

'By knocking that coward off his throne. In the name of justice; in the name of Aurabel!'

Lorali

A COW-SKIN RUG

'How did you know I was here?'

'You're everywhere. It's not exactly difficult.'

I see her flinch at that. It stings. I know. It's unavoidable. Her eyes out on the city view. Silence is the loudest mirror.

We are on the roof terrace of her penthouse. Watching the world like two angels. I couldn't have dreamt us up. How surreal this moment is. Who'd have thought that we'd be up here, us two tails, this high in the sky? The clouds blot the sweeping sky like an inky bruise. City lights illuminating Big Ben, wrapped up in gold like a bar of chocolate. The rooftops, spires of tiles, listen in on the reunion.

'How did you get here?'

'Train, of course. It's not hard, you know, Opal.'

'For you, maybe not.' She nods at my feet but I know she really means it's because she is too famous to get on public transport. Too far away from anything else. 'Did you tell anybody else you were coming?'

'No. I told them I was having swimming lessons!' I say, which is true. Even though I haven't swum since I left the sea for the last time. I can't. Not now I know Rory is in there somewhere and I'm not. That I've left him behind.

And, besides, swimming pools just aren't the same.

'And they bought that, did they?' she cackles and I shrug. None of my friends – well, the three that I have – *ever* ask about my swimming; they know not to. They know it's a deep crave that I push down like an alcoholic drives away a thirst. Impossibly necessary.

'Doesn't your water park open soon?' I ask, changing the conversation.

'How d'you know about that?' She seems embarrassed, like I am judging her for it.

'Again, you are *everywhere.*'

'Marco is doing a good job, I suppose.' She grins. 'Not until next month. I can't wait. I've got so many surprises planned . . . I'm . . .' She tails off before adding, 'Shall we get some bubbles? *Champagne?*'

'Tea's fine, thank you.'

'I'm going to have to order something in a minute, the fatty that I am.'

'You look great.'

'My arse is bigger than Myrtle's! *Please!*' She flips through the room service-menu. '*You* look great.'

I don't feel it. I feel like an alien dressed in 'girl' clothes. A fraud. Like a child forging their parent's signature.

I let Opal's eyes rest on me. I am sure she is curious. Peeling me apart. I almost want to get it out the way and undress for her, let her *see* my legs. Let her *see* everything.

'So what's it like then? Having legs?'

I haven't really answered this for myself. Sure, it is weird. New. Scary. Sometimes heavy. Sometimes painful. Sometimes tiring. But other times it feels like the only thing I've ever known – when my legs move without me thinking about it I realise it's me, just me.

'Freeing,' I say. 'It's freeing.'

Opal nods. Methodically sips the air in through her mouth, as if somebody has trained her to do it. 'Freeing. Now that's a word I like.' A tiny wind crawls over us, prickling our skin, in the natural way that skin judges a mood. She swigs pink wine from glass as thin as water, her plastic nails clamped around the stem like she's plucking a tulip.

I just have to ask her. The question is pressing on my tongue. Why is she dragging it out with the small talk?

'I hate to ask, Opal. But you're the only one who can help me.'

She sips again, smiling, eyes on her tail. Her tapestry is a new shade, unlike any of the Mers in the Whirl. The more she drinks, the deeper and more intense the colours become.

'Lorali, I could've helped you for the last two years. I could've made you a *star*. I wanted to help you and you *could* have helped me too. I asked you and asked you, repeatedly, *can you do this interview with me? Will you appear on this show with me?* Do you know what those freaks would do to get you? *Anything.*' Her voice rises. 'Do you know how *bad* it reflects on me to seem like I'm championing mermaids and the one mermaid who everybody *wants* to hear from doesn't want to speak to *me*? It's just embarrassing.'

'I'm not a mermaid, Opal.'

'Oh, get over yourself, Lorali. Just because you've got legs now – don't forget where you came from.'

'I have to remember every day where I came from.'

'Yeah, and it wasn't from here, was it?'

'Look, don't be angry at me just because I don't want the press in my face twenty-four seven; just because I want to live a life.'

'A life? I'm sorry, sweets, I love you, I do, but you don't live a *life*. HA! *This* is a life. Look – nice wine, cocktails, parties, clothes, look at this ring, look, this room, this view, this hair, this experience, the food, the people. *This here is life*. You could have it. For free. Lap it up. But you don't.'

'I don't want that. I want what I have. Normality. That's why I want you to help me, Opal. I know it's a risk. I know it's hard to go back, but I wouldn't ask you if I didn't need to.'

'Doll, I would normally, even if it's a risk, *anything* for you. But, trust me, I am helping you by saying no. There's nothing to cling onto in . . . bloody Brighton –

'Hastings.'

Whatever, Hastings. Even worse, OK? Nothing.'

'That's not true, Opal.'

Stay calm. I have to stay calm. I have to get her to go back for me. To find Rory.

'OK. It is great that you surfaced, had a little romance, *blah blah blah*, but that is *done* now. You've got that human being thing out of your system. Rory has gone. You can't spend the rest of your walking life hanging onto some guy you knew for a hot minute. Baby, you are *STUNNING*. You could have

104

any guy you want. You could *live* anywhere you want. And instead . . . you work in a fucking rundown lighthouse . . . err . . . where the light doesn't even *work*, with an old cray-cray lunatic who's basically banging on death's door and your ex-boyfriend's fucking pal who's *clearly* trying to sleep with you. And so, no. I'm sorry. I won't be fucking going down, back to that wretched, awful, rotten sea where those bitches shot me down. Because I am way up here. Making something of myself. And they are *down* there. And I never want to see them again. Not even if it is for you, Lorali. I won't.'

She reaches for her glass. And I look for my coat. But I can't find it in the bigness of the stupid room. All I can see is gold. Gold. And sparkles and shiny, shiny horror and mirrors. *Everywhere*. And the hugeness of the cow-skin rug – the skin of a living thing spread out on her floor as though it's art – and I feel sick and I can't find my coat still, but I don't care. I just want to be out of this room with this horrible mermaid and out of this hotel with the bright light and the beauty that I cannot touch and the world that I do not know and she is calling my name but I do not hear. My finger is on the button of the lift. My knees weak. That stupid publicist is waiting in the corridor. Calling my name too. Saying something unimportant. But I do not hear. And in the lift. With MORE mirrors. My reflection pinging back and I do not cry. Slow. I beat down the floors of the hotel. A woman with a yoga mat looks at me like I've lost my mind. Maybe I have. *Down. Down. Down.* I cannot wait to get home. I flood out of the open elevator doors. Rushing past. Fast. Suited people. Diners. Meetings. Briefcase. Cheesecake. Candle. Cocktails. Pearls. Glass. Puppies in handbags. Past reception. Hold the tears in.

All I want is home. All I want are my friends. All I want is Rory.

And I slip through the crowd of paparazzi, in and around the people, finding my feet. And then. I run. And I run. And I run.

And I never look back. Not once.

PART II

ONE MONTH LATER

THE SEA

TEARDROP

Aurabel, Aurabel.

Embraced by the solid arms of the bruised helter-skelter, now a browning tin where the candy-striped red and white has peeled. She can flop upside down, find living morsels clinging to the magic carpet, snooze like a kidney bean in the womb-like clutch of a waltzer buggy.

When a thunderstorm brings new waves Aurabel hides, finds shelter in the haunted house, where the clanking freaks can't judge. The bolts quiver, glass shatters, the rolling howl of terror raids, but she is safe. Eats fresh flesh of lobster claw and slurps razor clams and the roots of weeds where the nutrients are at their best. She lies on the ribs of a plastic skeleton in this welcoming house of horrors, placing her open hand where the heart would be. Seeking comfort in the obsolete. Talks to the screaming mouth of an old mad hag, babbling about her day like she's Murray.

Aurabel grows strong, understands that her hands are her

weapon. That she doesn't need two halves any more; she has become something new.

But, Aurabel, your Murray sleeps by the engine of a broken car, her crushed heart under the bonnet with the cold metal. She inhales you through the designs you've left behind. Softly mooned around the hardness that never seems to conduct the beats of warm blood. Some days she wants to give up. Not do a life without you. She feels the eyes of the others watching her drift along as a half. She feels so light she could bob away to the stars; without the weight of you to ground her she is helium. But then she is so heavy she could wrap herself up and drown in her own tears, cry until the ducts became crystals. Tears that compete with me to wash away the world and blind it to a watery melt of everything. And still she would see you in the mess of every angle. Aurabel, she thinks you are dead. That your bones lie in the grave of some monster's intestines; that it's coughing up blue hairballs, picking your ideas out of its teeth. Aurabel. Let Murray know that isn't true. Let her know you're coming home.

AURABEL

THE METAL TAIL

I don't breathe. I don't move. Not a muscle. I just watch. And wait . . .

BAM!

The bent hook drives into the heart of the ray. Using my arms I rake it towards me. Its wings flap helpless, then weightless . . . she's already dead.

Feel bad eating rays, a bit. Only because they're quite impressive. Did you know, when a ray gives birth, the baby pops out all rolled up? Like a scroll. It actually bursts out like that. And immediately, like the second it's out, it starts flapping. Unreal, isn't it?

It always gets me thinking about me. How I was born. Because we're not stupid. I know I was born up there. On some bed. Had some life before this one. We just don't get to think about it. And we certainly don't talk about it. But now I'm here. On my own. I can think about what I like. The gentle cotton folds of a mother. Maybe I had a father too.

A male has never held me before; the idea seems so foreign. My parents would be proud. They'd wrap their hands around my little foot and the sole of it would be soft, like moss. I guess they weren't to know they'd lose me. That's what I like to think. Whoever they are. Whoever they were.

Whilst I eat I crank up the puppets. Four little wooden Walker-like puppet dolls on strings that act out a band. They are so cute and cheery. If you wind up the crank at the back the band plays. One has a stick-like pipe thing, another a drum, one this set of strings and the other has this squeezy box that he pushes in and out. Course, the sound is almost completely muted – mostly bubbles just wheezily breathing out of the speakers. But if you listen really close, and imagine really hard, you can very nearly hear their music.

'Cheers, gents.'

After I eat the ray I get back to my tracking. Which is pretty much all I do all day, seeing as though that's all I can do until my strength is built up and I can move again. Tracking is a lot harder than it sounds . . . I do as many turns as I can on the wheel. It's hench. I can work out how it would've worked for the Walkers because there's these little carriages hanging on each spoke with a bar across. I think two of them Walkers would sit in each one. Still can't decide if this thing was made for pleasure or torture or transportation. Still, it works my arms up real nice. Obviously my bottom half is real heavy now, so the climb is hard. I clamber around the wheel, spinning it like a mill. The little carriages pick up water too, scooping it up as I go round – going against the current proper works your arms and core too. It burns.

Sometimes, I spin on the wheel for so long that I don't even know where the day has gone. It swims away and is dark before I know it. It's because I go into a trance, I reckon. Thinking about me. What I am now. My metal tail. Sometimes I still feel the skin of my tapestry, tingling. Like a phantom dull throb. The nerves wake me up in the night; I feel blood moving up and down the veins but they aren't real. Now I'm metal. Breathe in for six. Breathe out for six, five, four, three, two . . .

I think about Murray. About Tippi. About the king and how he probably thinks I just wasn't cut out for the job, like I shrimped out or something. Because that Sienna isn't going to tell the truth. And what will the Tips all be thinking about me? The rumours will be spreading, no doubt. And I think about other stuff too. Course I do. I have to talk myself out of the bad way and think about the positives . . . Like how I'm lucky to be alive. I think about how I'm gonna bounce back from this ten times stronger, a thousand times harder, than the Mer I once was. And then, and this is my favourite bit to think about (and nothing gets me working like this . . . so I save the thought for when I'm most tired and don't think I can manage another turn of the wheel), I think about how I'm going to kill Sienna. Rip her ribcage apart like an oyster shell; reach for her heart like the tiny black stone it is. And then feed it to her. And somehow the wheel always turns again.

113

Lorali

CHINA DOLL

Back in my home of Hastings, autumn's face has reared up in the form of sun-coloured fallen leaves and new seas. The air has a raw crunch to it. Deep craters of oily polluted puddles spoil the tarmac crosses of roads. Mothy overcoats and waxy macs roll out, smelling of cedar wood and attics, shoes with laces braving the boggy, moody hilltop.

Girls in town sniff me out. An arched eyebrow in a coffee shop stings me like lemon on a paper cut. Gangs of friends hang off park benches in gaggles, laughing at my attempts to be believable. Girls with low rucksacks and charcoal eyes, with piercings and coloured hair, girls with hard skin masked in cover-up, hip bones poking out. Girls who probably know how to growl.

Outside the chip shop a different gang of girls but girls all the same: drinking, smoking, singing. Lip gloss. Swamped in sweet marshmallow perfume and vanilla. A blinding mass of hot pink and neon yellow. Of trainers that are too cool for me.

Of jeans too tight. Full of stories I'll never get to hear, never get to retell. Songs I don't know. They snort when I pass.

I am unavoidable. Hard to miss. Even when I try to blend in I am always the one red sock in the white wash turning boys' cheeks pink. Which, in turn, makes other girls hate me. I can't go out. Not like other girls my age, because under crowded fluorescent blue lights I am a siren; a screaming alarm; a glitch. I don't know the words. I don't have the handbag. I don't have the right tickets or the right ideas. I don't tong my hair. I don't know the rhythm.

With eyes to the ground I walk forward everywhere I go. Only ever do what I came out to do. Get what I need. Talk to whoever I have to.

Until I can get back home again, where my shoulders can loosen, my knees can unlock.

I try to wash the thought of the Selkie away like a bloodstain on a sleeve. And the stain of Opal away even harder. Get back to the routine I know. For now, at least.

With a sense of normality readjusting itself, I get back on the familiar bicycle of life, pedalling breezily in the bliss of domesticated simplicity that I cherish so much. Trips to the supermarket with Cheryl to get milk, bread, bananas, eggs, wine, salad. The cinema with Flynn. And of course working at Iris Spy, where I happily while away the days scrubbing the dull bruised metal handle of an antique walking stick until it shines like a star.

I don't want magic.

I don't want any of the past to haunt me any more. I want to forget about it. The sea. My life before. And bury the world I once lived inside.

Until it finds me.

She seems kind enough as she snoops the shop; genuinely curious as she asks the price of a china doll. I never liked the doll myself. Her eyes are too silent. Of course she is a doll but she is unnerving; the seemingly content sassy smile and cocky expression across her face, as if she knows some inside secret she is leaving you out of – but if you gently knock her skull with your knuckle you're met with nothing but vacant echoes. She cheats you.

'Ten,' I say, hoping my voice doesn't sound too under-watery on its own without the voices of Flynn and Iris to counteract its telling tone.

'I'll take it.' She smiles, her eyes peering around the corner, as though checking to see if I am alone. Somehow she has a similar look to the doll. Just as beautiful, just as smug, just as secretive, although I doubt as empty.

'Would you like it wrapped?' I watch her wandering eyes glassily mesmerised by the cluttered walls of trinkets. Books, jars, pottery, wooden ornaments, tin toys, coins, jewellery, paintings, crockery.

'Oo, yes please, if you wouldn't mind?'

I reach for the newspaper and begin to happily wrap up this doll; I hide her face first so she can't say goodbye. The woman stands over me. Close. Suddenly, I knew exactly who this is.

A journalist. I know it. I can feel her. See her by a feeling, almost. I am cross now. I hope her stupid china doll smashes on the way home. *Why can't they just leave me alone?* I pick up the roll of tape, desperately trying to scramble for where the tape ends to get rid of her as quickly as possible, my fingertips skidding.

'Please,' she laughs. 'Let me help you with that – you need long nails for jobs like these.'

I say nothing but let her take the tape. Her fingers are elegant but one hand looks scarred: stitches seam up healed skin. Watching her . . . Black hair. Dark skin. Deep eyebrows. Green eyes. Long eyelashes. Who is she? She's wearing all black except for a grey leather jacket. And a scarf, with a pattern of single eyes dotted all over it. She bites the tape and makes me a perfect line, pressing it to my wrist and then another and then another. 'That should be enough.'

I smile shortly. Her leather jacket brushes against my skin, but doesn't feel like leather; it's . . . warm. She snaps up apologetically, bringing the jacket tightly around her, as though it has a life of its own and has to be reined in. She begins to browse, styling out her weirdness. I turn the radio up a bit to muffle the awkwardness. Jumpy music plays out in pirouettes.

'Oooo, what a *beautiful* coat!' She reaches for a big old fur thing. I've smelt it before. It stinks of dead animal. Warm blood. Of damp and decay. Not beautiful. Moth breakfast. So heavy it feels wet. 'Do you mind if I try it?'

'No. No, please.' I nod. 'There is a mirror just there but it's only small – I keep saying we should get a full length, but we just haven't got round to it.'

'Well then, I'll have to let you be my mirror! I trust your eyes!' She winks and wraps herself up into the furred skin. 'Well, what do you think?' She shrouds the coat around herself breezily, inside its swallowing bigness.

'I . . .' And then I smell her. Salty. The sea. She's the same species as the woman on the beach. I know it. I won't forget. She's a Selkie.

She rushes for me, seizing me in her grip, then pulls the collar tight around her throat, strangling herself with the neck of it and says, 'I can't talk. Not for long.' She wriggles words out of her mouth. 'It is not a safe time in the Whirl,' she spits. 'It is not as it was,' she adds quickly, but then, as if her voice is taken over by another's, just like with the other Selkie, she says, 'Rory is in danger.'

Not again. I want to be sick. I flush white. I need to be sick.

'Ignore me.' She shakes her head, again. 'There is still time to save him before his resolution. After he resolves you will not be able to but until then . . . you can . . . there is a chance.' Almost strangling herself with the collar of the coat, her hands clench, her eyes fix on me and they seem to water. 'Do not trust me; do not listen to anything I say. Keep your life here, as it is, Lorali. I've been sent from . . .' Flitting, she relaxes; resets her jaw with her hands, cranking it to one side. She collects herself once more. 'You have to save him.'

'How can I trust you when you keep contradicting yourself?' I am angry now.

'You can't.'

'So which one of you is telling the truth?'

'I can't say because you won't believe me, but one of us is Selkie and one of us is woman. I can tell you that other voice you're hearing isn't the truth. This voice you're hearing now isn't telling the truth either. I'm not lying. And the one who's telling you the truth isn't the one talking but the one who's silent isn't telling the truth. I am telling the truth.' I stare at this striking woman in the fur coat. Disbelieving that I've fallen into the trap of yet another Selkie and . . . this time . . . at my work. What next – will they come to my home? To Cheryl? Her eyes fix on me so hard they could bleed. My heart is in my mouth. Sickness in my gut. My skin tingles.

'OK. *If* I was to trust you and go back into the Whirl . . . say I don't make it – what happens then?'

The bell of the shop door tinkles open and Flynn and Iris enter with the cold, bold breeze and handfuls of shopping. The woman, startled, immediately jumps up.

'Not today, but perhaps I'll come back for it. What time are you open until?' She whips the bear coat off. Iris, in awe, double blinks at her beauty. It's the most pert I've seen him all week!

'It's a winner on you! You look a million dollars in it!' He beams.

'Oh, thank you. Perhaps I'll come back and try it again. It is getting colder. Summer's almost left the party,' she flirts. 'I really must be going.'

She slams the money for the doll on the table, wriggling herself out of the coat in a fluster before gathering herself out of the door. 'Thank you so much for your help. I hope to see you again soon!' She grins and winks at me. I feel Flynn's eyes looking at me to see if I'm OK but I'm not looking at him. I'm looking at the eyes on the scarf.

And I know what I have to do.

THE SEA

THE MISSING AURABEL

'Mer. My species. *My* kind,' Sienna hisses into the handheld tin cone, outside the palace gates.

Her hair is now ice-white in an almost solid high pony, her skin whiter. Snow-white brows and her filed fangs and split snake tongue make her serpent-like.

'I thank you for coming to the hearing today. Firstly, I want you *all* to know it is with a heavy heart that I appear before you today. As you well know, both Keppel and His Royal Highness, King Zar, are *friends* of mine of the closest nature. Watching them suffer as they went through the traumatic loss of losing their only daughter, Princess Lorali, was the hardest thing I have ever had to witness. Although I can appreciate this remains a distressing and heartbreaking struggle for the pair of them, I cannot sit back and watch as our beloved home, the Whirl, is misguided and led to its demise.'

The crowd of Mer listen attentively. A mix of Tips and Mer from the Whirl. Sienna has never been a council member they've warmed to – feared, yes – but they want to sound her out. Even her standing before them today is more than they have seen of Zar at all. Inside the palace, Kai is sent to his room, forbidden to witness Sienna's speech, ordered to turn his back on the circus below as the ringleader continues to weave her poison-laced threads of lies.

'Zar, I suppose, as any *desperate* male would when fighting a losing battle, panicked. He so badly wanted to unite the Mer and resurrect the spirit of community – but he employed an *inexperienced, young* orphaned Mer from Tippi town to clear out the forest. When he told me that Aurabel was to assist me, the keeper of beasts, of course I was elated to be partnering with the Mer of Tippi, whom I have always respected and admired. However, I was hesitant. I know only too well what the monsters of the water are capable of.'

At this, Sienna lifts her arm and rattles her wrist. The cuff clasped to the chain, link after link, the umbilical cord connecting her to the beast, Nevermind, is still. She smiles, ever *so* sweetly, and continues . . .

'I was wary, but, as just a council member I can only advise the king and ultimately the decisions always rest with him.' She holds her snide serpent tongue, pinning her words dramatically in the air. Kai cannot help but peer from his cut-out window, his heart beating. *What is this about?*

'Although this young Mer was a *fearless* and *talented* hunter, she was also a *domesticated*, generous *home* hunter – a raw hand. She wasn't trained or, dare I say it, *prepared* for the evils inside the depths of the forest. The *KING* gave young Aurabel *no* training, and no security, sending her out into dangerous open waters completely unsupervised. If I had known, I can assure you, I would not have agreed to it.'

Mer tut and coo, looking to one another. Some sob, for Aurabel. A few more Mer float towards the front. Angry Tips. Kai can't help but catch Murray's eyes. She came for his help. Did he let her down? She looks at him like he is guilty. He feels sick. She shoots her head down, stands closer to Sienna, unable to let her eyes meet the eyes of her fellow Mer. Or the eyes of the boy in the palace window.

'I now know from Aurabel's *widow* . . .' Sienna nods at Murray reassuringly, which invites a rearing sea of bobbing Mer heads to stare at Murray too. The dramatic word *widow* makes her want to collapse . . . 'that Aurabel was excited by this position. A job. A career. But also the wall of classes falling down, once and for all. Aurabel wanted unity. Attractive bait to be dangled, no? Any Mer would leap at the chance. But sadly, due to the king's ill-judgement and incompetence, his frail laws and own inexperience put that young Mer's fragile life in harm's way.' Sienna, milking the life out of her speech, theatrically takes an unbearably long pause. 'And Aurabel was attacked and eaten by savage monsters.'

Even though they've heard the rumours it does not stop the crowd of Mer from gasping. Kai's face creases in horror. Is this the truth?

'I do not want to be standing here in the future being told by the *weak* king to move in packs with weapons because the waters are not safe. Because the king is out of options. Because the king cannot keep peace, keep our waters under control. Or do his OWN dirty work! I do not want to be

122

standing here in the future being told that yet *another* Mer has died. NO!'

The crowd of Mer clap and applaud, cheering on Sienna's speech, which only encourages her to whip and fire her tongue even harder, even louder, even fiercer. 'Mer, I am unable to restrain the savage hunter inside my heart for *my* kind! I have to do what is right. I refuse to turn my back on you and leave you in the dark like your king is doing, and so I put it to you . . . I want to be the one, ME, standing here before you, to tell you that the waters ARE safe, that the Whirl is beautiful, peaceful, thriving and ALIVE!'

The Mer cheer, and Sienna smiles, glancing at Murray, who nods back in recognition, giving Sienna the confidence to scream her final point from the top of her lungs: 'I want to stand here . . . before you, Mer, as QUEEN!'

DNA MAG

THINGS TO DO THIS WEEKEND? Well, this week it's a no-brainer.

'Sleb' mermaid and party girl Opal Zeal raises the stakes again with the launch of her water theme park, GUSH! The style icon revealed that the park is a 'place to feel like a kid again' and added that 'lots of humans wanted to be mermaids when they were younger – and now they can in this experience!' But she warns that the park is 'like no other', with rides and attractions that promise to thrill.

GUSH is located in trendy East London's Hoxton and the dress code is 'splash with a flash' (whatever that means!). The slides appear to be like nothing you've ever seen before (imagine Picasso meets My Little Pony at an S & M party), apparently reflecting the true underworld life in the Whirl that Opal was once used to.

The word GUSH alone is trending! Hashtag serious FEAR OF MISSING OUT! The park is 12+ with a fully licensed bar serving Opal's FAVE cocktails and mocktails (warning: hot lifeguards) and is said to be more like a 'nightclub with water rides' rather than your average swimming pool. A secret special guest is rumoured to be performing live at the opening event! We think a spray tan, bikini wax and wedged-heel combo is a must. Guest list only. (OBVS.)

THE SEA

BOUND

Kai tears himself away from his bedroom window. He wishes he could have done more for Murray. Not Sienna. But he can't even help himself, let alone another. Why does his father have to be so lenient with everybody else but so strict with him?

If the council agrees to make Sienna queen – what does that mean for him?

What does anything mean to him?

As Kai rolls into his oversized scoop of a bed he feels an invisible lightness in his body. As fragile and as weightless as he realises he is. Unimportant. Invisible. Voiceless. He feels faint, like the haunt of a rumour.

What is this strange place? Why doesn't he feel like his name belongs to him? Why does he feel so old and young at the same time? So alive yet at moments like he is retracing a stranger's footsteps. Often his brain swishes and scribbles in a lucid state where he isn't sure what is real and what isn't.

Like waking from a dream. Has this always been his life? He remembers meeting Zar, the first face he ever saw . . .

'My boy, welcome home.'

Kai has no tangible reason to doubt his life as it is. That this is all there is. This is the only world, inside this palace, this place. This tight balloon. It is all so cloudy, but yes, there is some reminder in that enchanted secret wood, he is sure of it. It jogs a *something*. Like knocking a settled shell from a shelf and putting it back but not in the *exact* same spot. But he no longer knows where that shelf even is now that the forest hasn't opened. He has nothing to cling onto.

And now in the warped web of his head, textures and feelings wrap together. Scraps of his past like floating fragments twin up, but dissolve before he can make sense of them.

And even though he wrote the words 'I remember', he now remembers nothing.

When he resolves he knows his tapestry will have something to say. Then some story will be splattered across it in illustrative visions and perhaps something will make sense if it translates onto his scales.

And that's why he is looking forward to it.

MERMAID AND MERMEN APPRECIATION TRIBE – aka 'MAMAT'

This site is dedicated to the memory of Charlotte Wood. R.I.P. We luv u babe. We wil NEVA 4GET U. U wil ALWAYZ remain a mermaid in r eyes. <3 <3

MerBaby3000: LITRLLY BEIN SICK EVRYWHRE! OMG! K. K. K. LITRLLY PUMPED! Am so PLSD 2 announce tht Opal Zeal has askd MAMAT crew, aka ME, 2 attend the GUSH launch so we will b coverin the event so mke sure 2 fllw us 4 updates n newsfeed! We r litrlly ova the moon! Now . . . more importantly . . . WHAT 2 WEAR?

Vampfish: OMG! WELL JELS! FML!

FINFUN12:   GUUUUUSSSSSSSSSHHHHHING! I am going! CAN'T WAIT! Anybody else going? I'm coming all the way from France!

TwistedTail2: ONE WORD: GUSH.

Bellaseashella: OMG! GUSH LOOKS AMAZEBALLS!

TwistedTail2: Allow that word 'amazeballs' tho.

MermaidFanGirl_1:   **@MerBaby3000**   GASP!
PLLLLLLLLLLZZZZZZ LEMME COME W U!
BEB! PLZ!

TwistedTail2: Beggin' it u no.

Bellaseashella: @MerBaby3000 NOOOOOOOOO!
BUT SO HAPPY U GUYZ WILL B THERE U
TOTALLY DESERVE IT!

HDDNTRSRE: AHHHHHHHHHHHHHHHHHH! HOW
DO I GET TIX?

SWIM2DREAM: @MerBaby3000 WOW! LUCKY!

MYPERFECTTAIL: @MerBaby3000 @SWIM2DREAM
so SO LUCKY! I WUD DO NETHING 2 GO 2 GUSH!
LOOKS INSANE! DID U SEE THE PHOTOS OF
THE LAZY RIVA? MY ACTUAL GOD.

Vampfish: @MYPERFECTTAIL TOO MUCH! Looks
RIDIC!

MER-MUR: Why is **@MerBaby3000** going on like
'we' tho actin like theres sum big company crew of
you. We all no u is a 17 yr old girl from Essex sittin
in yer mum's kitchen actin like u sum big deal bizniz
woman ownin' sum empire. Pipe down love. Ur only
goin 2 a water park. CHILL. Big deal. Get ova urslf.

MerBaby3000: @MER-MUR BLOCKED!

TwistedTail2: BITCH! SHUT YO MOUTH JEALOUS H8TR!!! GRR!

MermaidFanGirl_1: GO BACK 2 UR WHACK FORUM @MER-MUR WIV UR 15 MISGUIDED FLLWRS. PLZ. LTRZ.

Vampfish: Evrybdy nos ur jealous of MAMAT success cos no one cares abt ur shit forum. U only steal MAMAT updates anyway. Recycled garbage.

SexSeaOpal: Note to self . . . a mermaid never loses sleep over the opinion of a prawn!

MermaidFanGirl_1: @SexSeaOpal 2 TRU. LOLZ!

MYPERFECTTAIL: Wonder what opal is gonna wear to GUSH. Wonder who the music act gonna be?! AGH!

MermaidFanGirl_1: SHE IS GONNA LOOK MEGA!

SexSeaOpal: Pray 4 weave!

Anonymous: I am sorry to gatecrash your site. I cannot say my name for confidentiality reasons. I have been living as a 'human' female in Germany for the past seven years. I have two children. I have been sitting on this secret for a very long time. When the mermaid revelation came up a couple of years back I felt like I was going to burst unless I said something. So here goes . . .

I was once a Selkie. If you don't know what one is see the link here . . . www.underwatersecrets.org/selkie+silkie+selchie

This is not a hoax. A lot to take in, I know.

I am never going back to the sea because we are treated like animals. WORSE than. There is no life for us in the sea. Opal Zeal paints a very pretty picture in the media that mermaids are *wonderful* and *beautiful* and *stylish* and *cool* and all the rest of it. But please do not believe what you read. I have never met Opal but I can tell you now the Mer species are very cruel to animals and other living creatures. They are NOT saving our planet, they are DEMOLISHING it! One Mer in particular – I used to live in fear, even up here, believe me, that SIENNA 'KEEPER OF BEASTS' (feels so good to have finally written her name down) would hunt me down and kill me, YES, even here, but after much support and encouragement – which took some convincing – from my husband and children and close friends

I am now confident enough to say it. This heinous witch claims to protect Selkies. She claims to 'house' us, and our babies, out of kindness. This is NOT TRUE. Sienna bribes Selkies to live on her land in exchange for protection from bigger beasts. The Selkies she keeps then have to live in tiny bunks in the worst conditions. She uses us as slaves. She beats us. She starves us. It is US who protect her but most of us are too afraid of her to see it. Luckily, I had no offspring as a Selkie, but if a Selkie has male pups the pups will be dragged away from the mother and sold off as guard dogs or hunters. It's DISGUSTING. This is why we are a dying species – nobody wants to reproduce because the babies will be ripped from our arms or we will live a life as a prisoner to a tyrant.

We are a rare and fragile species and Sienna dines out on that, forcing us to do despicable and unkind things. But nobody knows about it. I just want to say there are LOTS more women, trapped in the bodies of what seem to be 'seals' or 'walruses' and, even weirder, more women like me, who have escaped, now out here trying to live normal lives. Many Selkies cannot just simply give up their lives in the sea, not only because they are petrified or trapped but because they have their pups to care for. This is a desperately sad situation that has been ignored for TOO long. I am writing to your site in the hope that you share this and spread the word. WE NEED A PLATFORM!

One final request: please can you stop promoting mermaids until you have your facts straight. They are a heartless and cruel species. And I'm not going to sit in silence any longer. IT'S TIME FOR CHANGE!

MYPERFECTTAIL: Errrr . . . what the frig was that about?

SexSeaOpal: DID I JUST REALLY READ THAT?

MYPERFECTTAIL: Tres awks.

SWIM2DREAM: Flip! **@Anonymous** who r u?

MYPERFECTTAIL: **@SWIM2DREAM** if she says she's anonymous it means she's anonymous. FFS. DUH! READ!

SWIM2DREAM: **@MYPERFECTTAIL** Calm it Kermit! I was only askin.

WhereisLorali: Shit, so is this tru?

SexSeaOpal: Ask @MerBaby3000

STARTHESTARFISH: I wanna dye my hair blue, thoughts?

MerBaby3000: Hi guys, srry, jst seen ths. Cmpltly shckd. Wot? Dunno wot 2 do.

Vampfish: CALL THE POLICE!

MermaidFanGirl_1: In my opinion u hve 2 help this woman, she is clearly having a mental breakdown. @MerBaby3000

Starryfish: @MerBaby3000 u must help her immediately, it seems to be a very pressing matter that needs attending to urgently so give me your GUSH ticket and I'll go along on your behalf. LOLS! ;)

MermaidFanGirl_1: @Starryfish NICE TRY!

WhereisLorali: LOOOOOOOONY!

MerBaby3000: K, I jst googled Selkies – 'mythical creature' hlf woman, hlf seal fing. Shit. So this woman lives here now?

SexSeaOpal: @Anonymous can JOG ON! HOW

DARE YOU B WRITING ABOUT MERMAIDS LIKE THAT? Opal Zeal is an absolute QUEEN! WHO THE HELL EVEN ARE YOU COMING ON HERE SPEAKIM ABOUT MERMAIDS LIKE THAT? I'M GONNA SET MY DAD ON YOU.

SexSeaOpal: Typo *SPEAKIN even. How embaz. FML.

Sailortailor: @SexSeaOpal LOL! PREACH!

FINFUN12: SELKIES SUCK!

Sailortailor: Did @Anonymous not read the friggin GUIDELINES? This is a <u>mermaid appreciation society</u>, not a seal one, go to Sea Life mate.

MerBaby3000: Nt guna lie tho squad, I am sooooooo gasssssssed that my blog has reached Germany! How du say 'ello in German then?

MermaidFanGirl_1: I'm having nothing to do with this and it's not even my business but if I was u @MerBaby3000 I wud take this woman n get her 2 a therapist or something ASAP. ☹ Pretty sad story. Made me quite emosh.

SexSeaOpal: Or just delete the comment.

MerBaby3000: Ur rite. Ths is kinda killin my vibe rite now tbh. Deleting it now. Looks well bad 2 new coMer dunnit? Srry **@Anonymous** but there's a time n a place and it rlly ain't now.

THE SEA

THE SABRE TOWER

In the jagged rotting tooth of the Sabre Tower I breathe. Sharpening her teeth like the jaw of a shark, Sienna is teaching her first salvaged the art of a campaign. A new young one she has housed for a while. In secret, of course. He is a smart thing, learning his way of the world in the syrupy blackness that Sienna calls home. She has named him Victor. Often Sienna, as she watches him wading about their tower, talking and learning and asking questions, thinks of him as more than a son . . . more than a young man . . . Sometimes he is too beautiful to be a son . . . sometimes, in the dead of night, she thinks about other ways they could become closer, other ways she can reach him, taste him . . . and new ways that he could reach her? Taste *her*. She doesn't *have* to resolve him as her son; could she resolve him as her mate? After all, there is a shortage of the things. Or perhaps that is forbidden. Or perhaps that's why she is so grotesquely hungry for him. *Because it* is *frowned upon . . .*

One doesn't tessellate with one's salvaged. That's pretty much the only rule of Mer tessellation.

But maybe if she could have him, just once, she wouldn't want him quite so much. If ever she puts the idea to bed she only needs to be reminded by the architecture of his body: naked shoulders, strong back, spine. The idea stirs inside her, obsessing over his size and shape and hands and neck and chest.

All those discoveries would be decorated onto him. And all those messages. All those painted scars and all that history. Maybe he doesn't even need to be resolved at all. He doesn't need a tapestry. His body says it all.

Anyway. She could be queen soon . . . *Then*, in her own words, *she can do what the hell she wants.*

The Selkies flump in the entrance. *Fat fucks.* She likes them so much better like this. When they are not beautiful and threatening but wobbling. Blubbering. Oversized hefty morsels.

'Well?' Sienna spits. 'Did you do well?'

The Selkie in question has a flipper that has been snagged by a fish hook. You might know her from the land as a beautiful woman with a scarred hand. She flops to the ground in relief, but solemnly heavy; her heart sinks for what she has done.

'Do not look so sad, Selkie. You've done your job, you will be rewarded handsomely, and you and your little pups will continue to be protected in return.' Sienna pats the head of the Selkie; the others look on, trembling, all feeling the imprisoning weight of oppression. 'Perhaps your pups will eat tonight.' Sienna weaves between them menacingly. What a fine villain this Mer is becoming.

The Selkie in question begins to weep. Sienna tries to tickle their chins but her tickle comes in the form of a spiky scratch. 'Poor, poor things. Must be hard to be so beautiful and charming on land . . .' Sienna inspects her claws. 'Then ugly, fat, mute and useless down here. What brutal punishment for all the lies you spin on land. Such a shame,' she snarls sarcastically. 'But know that *luckily* you've *finally* come to some good. When Princess Lorali dares return, yes, when she's bobbing on the head of the sea, when her chunky Walker legs sink her down to fish food, when her clothes become rags, when her bulky bones clunk like an anchor, yes . . . when she's *dead*. HA! Devastating news like that will shake the palace gates. News like that *will* crack Zar's composure and boot that sad whelk off the stand once and for *all*, and I will be queen!'

And she cackles demonically up into the green waves, like the terrible fairy story witch that she seems to have become.

And I know all of this sounds very pantomime, but that's the wonderful thing about narrating a fairy story like this. You can be as dramatic as you like. And I am the sea, after all. I love a bit of drama.

Lorali

ONLY THE END

Humans are funny creatures. Funny things who sit cross-legged on floors when there are empty chairs around. Funny things who don't say what they mean. Who would rather struggle than ask for help. Who eat hot chips even when they know they will burn the mouth. Funny things who smoke poison. Who don't help themselves. Who run even when they are not being chased. Humans listen to music in their ears through little buds on wires and they don't sing along. They don't dance. OR nod their heads. Humans copy each other. With clothes. With taste. With ideas. Humans pick up the poos of dogs with little bags.

Humans think everybody is lying to them. The ones who are lying are the ones the humans give their money too. Humans forget there is choice. Even though they have too much of it. Humans get flustered. And don't speak. And don't listen. Humans stare at the phones and miss the sun. The stars. A smile . . . maybe even their children putting out a small hand to them. Some humans don't even share but stare. Instead. Humans would rather write it down than say it out loud. They cry in films when people are acting. And they know they are acting. They get angry for people who are not them. They get scared of things that are not real. Nervous of things that have not yet even happened and probably will not. Humans forget to laugh sometimes, forget to listen, watch, be patient, be kind, be curious, eat when they are hungry, drink when they are thirsty, explore. They have forgotten what this is all for. Humans are funny creatures.

We eat at the lighthouse. Cheryl comes too. Crusty white bread and salty butter. Brown stew with carrots and heaps of tea and red wine. Creamy mashed potatoes and orange swede. I eat and eat even though I am not hungry. I want to weigh myself down. Heavy with wine. I watch the people I love laughing and talking. Iris plays his records. We have blueberry loaf with cream cheese frosting for afters. Flynn's cheeks are red from the heat of the oven. Iris forces me to dance with him. I feel like I am dancing with a god. He spins me around and around until I'm dizzy, thinking of what I'm losing, what I've lost. I want to cry in the closing drunken stupidity of it all. How foolish I was to think I could make this work for me.

I want to tell them all that I'm going. And I don't want to. I want to tell them that I love them. That I might return with Rory but I don't want to get their hopes up. So I can't. I don't say a word. Eyes closed. I fill every gap in the air with the sound of laughter.

Cheryl sings. She is tipsy. I smell her perfume-rich music notes in the air and I run through the scented mist, letting the rich, wet, floral dots of her rain down on me. Cheryl dances with Iris. They hold each other. Tight. Just as a replacement. They are thinking of other people. I think about how weird I am that this is how I spend my last night. How different I am from other girls my age who would rather be getting drunk in a club somewhere. I don't want to change. Flynn and I wash up together. Red knuckles in clouds of fairy liquid. Dishes squeak. I'm drying up. And then I dive my hands into the water. Right up with his. And squeeze his fingers so tight.

'What are you doing?' he laughs.

'I just wanted to hold your hands.' My voice is slow and breaking but embarrassed.

'Weird girl.' He carries on scrubbing. 'You're drunk, silly.'

I remove my hands and then he quickly dries his on his T-shirt but it isn't a long enough dry to make his hands actually dry and then he gathers me up and squeezes me hard into a hug. Tight. His wet handprints leave palm-shaped scars on my back and dress. And I let tears fall. And it's almost as though he knows what I'm going to do that night. And he's OK with it. And even if he doesn't know, then that's what I'm going to pretend to myself. That he knows. And that he's OK with it.

Fully clothed, to make me feel safer. The sleeping grey sea. The water is slashing me numb already. The ice crowds me. Iris's ocean eyes. The water tickles my skin like ghostly spiders climbing my limbs. I hear the voice of the sea in shushes. Go. *Don't go*. Walk. *Don't walk*. Deeper. COME. Deeper.

I selfishly grip to my life. Arms out to the sides, like a tightrope walker. White moon. The bright, drunken twinkles of the fading beach I'm leaving behind. Human shouts. Wonderful world, don't go. I walk in until the pebbles that scratch my soles turn to sand. Relief. Shivers. Hairs on end. Nipples. Shock shooting up. Wired. Electric. Beating. Throb.

And my clothes soak. My skirt billows. Out like a parachute and then the water dampens it. Chasing the drench. Darkening the colour. Hair starts to get wet. Salty. In my eyes. Heavy from the food and alcohol but that weight seems to have worn. Too cold. Too scared. Too sad. *Rory*. The water begins to push me back. But I'm up to my throat. The hands of the waves rummage. Spikes crystallise . . . salty ice fingers strangle and lick. Bruising me with depth and danger. Heart – *smash. Smash.* Body light. Start swimming. Am I? Can I? Mouth. Salt. Sting. Eyes. Ocean on ocean and its many layers. As weightless as a polystyrene coffee cup thrown off the pier. Dissolving like a tablet on the tongue of a giant.

Hello, old friend. Hello, little Lorali. Yes, I think I can remember you, child. You don't know me any more . . . but I know you well.

I've been waiting for you.

THE SEA

WELCOME HOME

Of course we knew Lorali would drown. And she did.

A Mer, once surfaced with legs, can never come back down. We all know that. Otherwise the greedy things would be up and down for ever. But Lorali is no ordinary Mer. Half and half. One of a kind. It happened when her body immersed, reaching the tip of the Whirl. That was where the true magic happened. (I may have pushed her along slightly, but that's by the by. It was inevitable, and what did you expect me to do, reader, leave the girl a dead raft? Don't be ridiculous. I owed it to this brave girl to make it down, at least.) And so it was: her tapestry formed. The legs gone immediately. Just a simple slip of a tail for now – she never was fully resolved, was she?

So she remains silver. Still natural. A newly formed tapestry that reminds me of whale blubber in texture but it's a little more translucent, like skin. Though it's a misty fog, like trapped smoke in a jar, almost yellow, like fingernails, like shells, like candle wax. After the resolution you can see the spirits of a personality dancing about, fluttering like coloured smoke, like feathers, like seaweed. The older the tapestry, the more these illusions begin to stain, impressionable marks like tattoos or birthmarks that become for ever.

And here she is, a new thing once again. And the movement of the tail, it startles, rousing . . . begins to flip and spasm awake and is swimming and thrashing. Like the lost control of a speedboat engine. Clapping my body, wanting to dart all over.

But why her soul is not where her tail is I do not know.

Live, little fish. You have come too far, hurt too hard, loved too sweet to lose now.

But she is not there. Lorali is dead.

There is nothing that I can do except take the girl and her tail to the bottom of the bed.

It is a sad ending. Her head fills with air. Her eyes close. Her chest collapses. Her lungs fill with water. Her ribcage snaps. Her heart stops. Blue in colour all over. Just like me. The tail eventually falters, spasms, stops wriggling.

Half Mer, half Walker. Half alive, half dead.

The Selkies, who have been forced to watch Lorali's movements, holler when they spy the drowning. They call her with their song. Sienna watches with a telescope, high in her tower, her snooping third eye of interference. And then she flees to the scene to ensure the job is done. Hiding behind a snag of rock, she watches her friend's daughter losing her breath.

Fuck.

She wasn't *meant* to grow a tail. That is the last thing Sienna expected. Nor is this sinking to the bottom of me wanted, the

145

smashing of a head and bleeding, unconscious, coffin bones and flesh for fish food.

And it is so graceful, Lorali's death, like a paper lantern. Sienna twitches with a pang of bitterness. Perhaps Lorali is more of a miracle that even *she* anticipated.

But wait . . . their eyes *lock*.

'Help me, Sienna. Sienna . . . it's me, Lorali.'

For one small crumb of a second it happens . . .

But Sienna ignores the begging. She tucks herself in, back against the wet rock. *Be silent. Do not move.*

And when she can bring herself to look round again.

It is done.

THE SEA

MUDDY WATERS

Naturally, Marcia snarls at Sienna when she bells the gates of the palace.

'Do NOT let her in!' Zar roars at his mate. 'Do not let that traitor in our home.'

'She has urgent news for us, Zar.'

'It's a trap.' Zar rips at his scalp with blunt nails. Knotting his frazzled grey beard into rope-like twists.

It is Keppel who releases the guards and grants Sienna entry.

A snake is Sienna, worming her way back inside the hearts of old friends by the doors of their home, carrying the cruel gift of bad news.

Now, as Bingo fixes them a smoke and sea-nettle tea, Sienna speaks as genuinely as her voice can tremble.

'My darling friends,' she begins, ignorant in believing she can begin where she left off – but she is wrong.

'You are not our friend, Sienna,' Zar's voice booms in reminder. Little Kai jumps at the power of his voice – this tone does not belong to Zar. Terribly out of character.

'Zar!' Keppel throws him a glance, also surprised at his rage.

'I am sorry you feel that way, Zar, but this is why I've come.' Sienna does not flinch. Back straight. Poised.

'I don't want to hear anything you have to say,' Zar rips. 'One moment you are our friend, the next you are shoving a trident of betrayal into my spine to get me off the throne. That *speech* you gave outside my gates was lies and you know it. Yet you still want to come into our home and call us *friends*. I don't think so, Sienna,' he bites. 'Now get out!'

Rattling chinaware, the palace quivers. Keppel rakes her hair with her hand, bringing it over to her mouth to stop herself from telling her mate to calm down. *Why isn't Sienna reacting? Normally she'd be firing her tongue right back at Zar . . .*

But today Sienna holds hard, difficult to tremor, relaxes and says quite frankly: 'I want to let you both know that I am stepping down.' This is a lie, her personality a cream already curdled sour. 'I don't want to fight you for your crown, Zar.'

Keppel looks saddened still that the crown is a loss to her; her mother would've been disappointed. 'You don't have to step down, Sienna,' she says softly.

'Yes I do. I want to talk openly with you. Putting the Whirl and the council on ice, can we just be ourselves? I have something I need to tell you,' Sienna whispers, very convincingly. The tea enters but Zar won't have any of it.

'No tea. NO! Get out!' Zar snaps. He paces the room, his face a messy map of tangled roads and misleading veins. 'Sienna, the damage is done. You're toxic. I don't want you near my family, do you hear?'

'It's about Lorali.'

And they sit. Even at her name they weaken. And they try to listen. Of their lost baby daughter who is now lost for good. The frayed edges of hope they had tattered together splatter into torn scraps.

Keppel's cries ring through the palace. Such a weary, frail thing she has already become, and this terrible news blitzes her brain to sand. For the first time in what seems like ever, she throws herself into the arms of her mate, Zar. He holds her tight, their wails in waves, their embrace laced in the fuzzy music of broken sobbing, rippling like my waters on a calm day. Peace of mind is always a light at the end of any tunnel.

'At least she died a Mer.' Keppel strokes her lover's beard and wraps her small hands inside his. 'She was trying to come back to us. She knew it was an impossible feat, but did it all the same.'

Red eyed, Zar nods. 'I shall retrieve her body myself –' he wipes away his tears – 'and bring her home. Where she wanted to be.'

Sienna hadn't anticipated that he might suggest this, but of *course* he would want to retrieve his dead daughter's body – why didn't she factor that in? She is too deep inside a lie now. She shakes her head. 'I already went out with my monsters, myself, so you didn't have to go through the pain, and I'm afraid . . . she's . . . not there.' Sienna clasps her slim hands to her chest.

'Oh, Zar, my heart, no!' Keppel throws herself into Zar's lap and sobs.

'No, it's OK, Keppel. It is fine. It is better this way; it would hurt too much to see her still.' Zar weeps. 'This must have been very hard news for you to break, Sienna. We are grateful.'

Sienna darts her eyes to her tapestry, which flashes a violet, deep, hideous purple, immediately exposing her darkness.

Oh, Sienna. You lie.

Kai watches Zar and Keppel. *Why are they crying? Who is lost?* Who is the painting of the girl on the palace wall? Has she *died*?

And now they are so close, these two isolated shapes that drifted the palace like strangers. The fog of tension that kept them apart suddenly seems lifted in a moment. And now as they cling together, it seems every part of their bodies has to be touching or else they will stop breathing. What are *Walkers*? Who is that? Aren't they *all* Mer?

The palace, even with the bad news, manages to find relief in the closing of a painful chapter. And as sea leaves turn, old lovers become new again inside the palace walls; the lights come on. Twinkling splatters of mirror that make the palace shine up the Whirl, as though they have stolen the moon itself and harvested its fat beacon in my waters. It seems Lorali is no longer lost; she has been let go of.

. . . Leaving Kai with the scrambled clues. He can't stop thinking about Lorali.

How much she is missed by the Mer in the Whirl only makes Kai wish he'd had the chance to meet her. Because she must have been very special.

AURABEL

ONE MER AT WAR
WITH THE WORLD

I know I am ready.

I'm done with my track running – looping around the nutty hoopy thing so hard I tasted blood in my gums and my veins popped out of my wrists.

I am gonna kill them monsters that tried to kill me. And after that, I am gonna take down the biggest monster of them all. Si-fucking-enna.

The actions I do are all planned. I've had weeks to think them through, lying in the silent stillness, going through every range of rage. Because, you know what? I am *glad* I've been gifted this challenge. I am *grateful* for it. Because there aren't many of us who are strong enough to take a thing like this on and obviously something in my stars thinks I am. So THANK YOU. No more crying and punching and feeling sorry for myself. I can think straight now I've got used to it. Got stronger for it. Own it. I've taken this anger and now I've hard-boiled it down to a roaring fire pit in my gut and I'm using it, but it has to be monitored, drip-fed to me in doses. Like, I can't just use all the fire in my belly at one time because firstly I'd explode and secondly because I don't want to use it all up in one go. This fire, this bright flame of anger, is what's kept me going. Now. I fight. I can roar. I am strong. I can fucking swim. And I ain't just any old Mer from Tippi now – I'm half metal, mate. And ready for revenge.

I shave my hair off with a razor blade I make from bruised and battered steel. Now, I know this seems extreme but I'm not the Aurabel I once was and I can think of far better uses for this barnet than it being on my head. Plus, it is proper recognisable and I don't want to get seen once I'm ready to leave here. I use metal scraps from the same steel as a mirror. Hacking off the thick blue hair, which is so long, by the way, with the razor at a blunt angle. I make a little fringe. Just to see how I'd look.

Too psycho bitch? Yeah, probably. I smile. I was known for my hair. But I'm not known any more. With each cut comes lightness. It is like I suddenly feel so light, I could float to the surface like a bubble. That hair went on for ever, heavy wet rags – how'd it grown so much? Can't believe I carried that load with me so long.

With the hair hacked short enough, I take the razor at a new slanted angle and cut close. I accidently cut my scalp a couple of times but they are only nips. I won't be satisfied until I've seen every turquoise strand of hair off my head. Until my head is dotted grains. Smooth like a pebble. When I'm done comes the next bit.

152

I take all the strands of hair I've chopped off and I sit and I don't move, not until it's done. Under the coloured mini lamps of the sea-bugs I am able to work. I knit all the strands together. I'm making a net you see. And it has to be big.

THE SEA

THE SENSITIVE
SOUL OF A SELKIE

You remember the Selkie with the ragged flipper who visited Lorali in Iris's shop? Ah, well . . .

The sensitive soul of a Selkie sits like foam on my surface. That Selkie knew Lorali was a love-sickly girl only trying to start again in a Walker world without the one Walker she truly loved. This Selkie lied to Lorali. She watched her fall from her life to her death. She said she would be safe. This Selkie acted ugly for insurance. The promise of safety. That her babies and her kind would be protected from monsters. From storms. From icy waters. From poachers and hunters and those with the proddy sticks. But there was no protection from Sienna herself. You cannot trust somebody who mistrusts the rest of the world. Now, when this Selkie sees the palace ablaze with the crystal dazzling lights, this Selkie is sickened that Lorali *trusted* her enough to give herself back to me. And that it was her fault. She was plucking a death march on that young one's heart strings.

The guilt is too much. And the mistrust. And the doubt. And the struggle; the only thing this Selkie hates more than Sienna is herself. She cannot live with a guilt like this.

This Selkie takes her pups and leaves them to sleep in the bed of a friend. Soon they will know that I am not the only place for them. That there is the whole world.

With weeds, she makes a knot for a noose. Here she dangles, asleep, like a helpless fish at the end of a rod. Where the guilt cannot kill her the slow way.

AURABEL

A FISH IN A NET

Steering myself, I glide at rapid pace through the choppy waters. The turquoise veil made from my hair hangs like a bridal train behind me, streaming like liquid. I hurdle and duck and dive with the compass of my instinct. I am out in the cold open waters that offer me things. I almost seem to recognise where I am. Maybe? Dunno. I start to feel sick. Like the memory is coming back. Is my brain not ready? Doing all that over-thinking. I see the serpents again in my head, big things, teeth, reaching out, hurling me, so quickly. Every shadow is a blade aiming for my chest. Calm. Six, five, four . . .

Wait. Wait. Wait. Who is that?

A Mer. Female. Crashed against the rocks, she sleeps, so heavy and motionless. *Hold on.*

I know this face.

'Shit the seabed, it's Lorali. The princess.' I press my fingers to her chest, her heart: still. I look around for somebody to help . . . the palace is so far; my brain is so revved. I can't just . . .

And before I know it I am swimming back the way I came. To our isolated adventure land, with a princess over my shoulder whose heart has stopped beating.

THE SEA

GUSH

'And it gives me –' *hold the smile. Hold the plastic lip-gloss smile –* 'enormous pleasure to announce that GUSH, the first ever naturally salted, mermaid-themed water park, is officially OPEN to the public!' A rainbow ribbon is cut. People applaud. Press take photographs. *Snap. Snap.* Bright, brilliant, blinding light. *Blah, blah, blah* and more *blah.* Champagne corks and YAY. OMG. CONGRATS. LOLZ.

Does Shoreditch *really* need a water park?

Apparently so.

A rapper spits aggressively into a microphone on a free-standing faux island about 'her money'; electric currents hiss through the wires, keeping her voice alive. Water and sparks don't mix, if you ask me. Nobody *ever* asks me. This should be fun.

What can only be described as 'buffoons' rush into the tarted-up leisure centre. A gaggle of screaming . . . *youngsters* leaping and being OMG *excited.* A mirror ball spins, chucking twinkling diamonds on my body below. A new sea of dry ice hangs over in a mist and makes me heavy. I appear moody, swampy, but that's what they like, these big kids in their vintage swimming costumes, their platform boots (at the swimming pool?), their sunglasses (we are indoors), their wings and wigs and caps and fake Mer-tails and glitter and sequins and lipsticks. It's comical. I have seen nothing like it. I *wish* she'd gone with chlorine. Then I wouldn't have to be here watching this mess. Spilling bodies, rolling out of ill-fitting neon numbers, brightly coloured two-pieces made for anything *but* swimming, which is fortunate as nobody is doing any *swimming*.

'THIS IS SICK!' Marco screams over the music as he and Opal watch from the glass viewing box. One hand on his child-sized bony hip, the other balled into a fist, thrusting into the sky like he's cheering on a fight, a ballerina lightfoot attempting an out-of-tune *stomp* to the beat. His fake tan streaking brown smudges on the toes. 'I can't believe we actually got her to come. Look, the press are *lovin' it*!' Opal nods whilst she watches the big adults take selfies and dance to the music. She is watching their legs. Their ankles. Their toes. Their shoes. Their hips. Their knees. Their calves. Their thighs. Their thigh *gaps*. Is she really going to do this?

'FYI!' Marco squeals. 'They've opened up the slides! It's almost time!'

A tangle of brightly coloured slides hangs in the air, shooting off into all directions in the vast building and curving out of it too, so that riders can watch the envious media folk charge to work.

There is the Big Drop, an almost vertical slide that plunges its victims from a great height into a deathly freezing pool of ice

159

water (I mean, *they* don't know the meaning of *ice cold* water but I don't want to patronise). The plunging pool has been designed like the Arctic, so you can enjoy being roared at by a glittery robotic polar bear, and growled at by a mechanical snow leopard.

There is another ride called the Mermaid's Kiss, a smooth trip into the open mouth of a model mermaid, where riders wriggle into a mermaid's-tail foam mat, dangerous for foot cramp but *wow* are *they* popular. Inside, strawberry- and champagne-flavoured bubbles float, hideous music *plonky-tonks* from speakers and there's more of that dry ice. Riders can kiss the mouths of tacky models dressed as mermaids, receiving drink tokens for the bar, almost as reward for doing absolutely nothing.

You could try the Fire Pit, a steamy sauna slide, which apparently detoxes your skin as you retox your gut on the tequila shot you neck before hurling yourself and your inhibitions into the throat of the slide.

No, don't fancy it – not for you? Why not try the Lost Lagoon, a soupy horror underwater slide of a ride that features quicksand and the snapping jaws and claws of 'monsters'. 'ARGH!' they scream. *Monsters? They don't know the meaning of the word*.

The Mud Slide is exactly as it reads, and then there's the Lazy Boy River where you can have a chocolate milkshake and play computer games whilst floating on the waterproof pads.

But best is Opal's *Riviere Noir*. A pitch-black chute, lit only by the UV paint that the users choose to splatter themselves and each other with beforehand. Naturally, left to these apes, you can imagine the acid-green handprints on breasts and bottoms. Lots of dipping fingers and wedgied bum cheeks. But that's all part of the fun, isn't it?

'It's time!' Marco shrieks.

Opal feels sick. She is really about to do this, isn't she? It is too soon. She still aches. It is all happening so fast.

Her security carries her to a perch at the top of the *Riviere Noir* as the lights go down. The humans scream! The UV lights up. And the music stops. Completely.

The rapper in the mic shouts, 'Please . . . allow me to *reintroduce* to you, breaking history, the one and only, the global sensation that is . . . Miss Opal Zeal!'

'AAAAAAHHHHHHH!' the fans scream; they can't believe it, a REAL mermaid! Drinks and cameras at the ready, they fight to the front. Elbows, arm bands, blow-up flamingos . . .

And down she flies, out of the slide, rebirthed into the salt lake of the pool beneath: Opal Zeal. The lights come on as she lands. A washed-up mermaid.

But this time . . .

She has no mermaid tail. She is wearing legs.
SURPRISE!

MERMAID AND MERMEN APPRECIATION TRIBE – aka 'MAMAT'

This site is dedicated to the memory of Charlotte Wood. R.I.P. We luv u babe. We wil NEVA 4GET U. U wil ALWAYZ remain a mermaid in r eyes. <3 <3

THS IS ACTUALLY THE WRST DAY OF MY NTIRE LFE. NO JKES. NOT EVN FNNY. LITRLLY. Waiting 4 sum1 PLZ 2 tll me tht this is sum EVIL screwd up April Fools prnk n it ain't even APRIL!

NO! NO! Wht the actual earth is gng on? Im sry bt no! Cnt evn tlk. So dpressed. Opal Zeal is selfish. I will neva 4get what she's done 2 me. Afta all I hve dne 4 her. Litrlly fl so betrayd rite now. I am done. LEGS! L-E-G-S! LEGS! WTF? WT THE ACTUAL F? I can't. I literally can NOT. Can I live? No. Dead. Goodbye.

> **MermaidFanGirl_1:** I have no words. Literally like not a single word. But OMG. Thre I am literally waiting 4 my Frapps in Starbucks and wot do I see? What on earth was she thinking? Did she have SURGERY? What kind of INSANE DKHEAD doctor performs such an operation on somebody so perfect? WTF?

Vampfish: @MermaidFanGirl_1 Must have been paid a LOT of money.

OpalsBFF: I think it's so sad that she felt she had to conform. Society puts such pressure on us to look exactly the same – like robots. Like we have to be so tanned and skinny and have big lips and big bums and big boobs and a manicure. It's exhausting and it's unrealistic. AND expensive! Celebrity culture is even worse. Even more pressurised. Look at the magazines. They are constantly drawing those red circles around her bum all the time. It's like 'errrr she has a TAIL!' She probs just wanted to fit in. And now she's JUST the same as everybody else. The one thing that made her special is now gone. She's no different from the rest of us. Devastated.

SexSeaOpal: The magazines have a LOT to answer to. TRAGIC!

TwistedTail2: Wonder where her tail has gone? I am CRYIN MY EYES OUT.

FishOUTofH2O: WHAT IS THE POINT OF ANYTHING ANY MORE? FML. FML. FML.

SexSeaOpal: @TwistedTail2 so true. Pbs in sum dustbin sumwhere. Let's go find it. I wud LITERALLY sew it 2 my own skin.

MYBABELORALI: Sry but I am unsubscribing. Mermaids no longer exist. Full stop.

Vampfish: I just watched the clip from GUSH online. She looks hot. But the scars look bad. Ouch. The legs are fresh tho!

WhereisLorali: I am takin the day off school for this shit.

Vampfish: DESIGNA VAGINA!

CoralCaroline: *designer

MermaidFanGirl_1: @Vampfish obvs hasn't healed yet. Imagine having half your body chopped off just for the sake of fashion. Yikes.

Vampfish: Apparently Opal stones are bad luck! Just saying!

MerBaby3000: Does anybody have a contact for **@Anonymous** if so can you DM me?

CoralCaroline: This is so fucked. You lot love this.

THE SEA

A CROWN WITHOUT
A HEAD

Another small council meeting takes place in the gardens of the palace. A plush stretch of seagrass and water lilies, orchids and silver bells sprinkle the perimeter. A monument, which happens to be what Walkers use to keep their fires inside . . . a *fireplace*, I believe is the term for it (although how Walkers keep a fire inside one's home without burning the whole place down, I will never know), is the centrepiece for the meeting.

Myrtle is first to arrive. She has made honeycomb from sap and brought it in blocks that look like crumbling gold. They need sweetening, these bitter Mer. She holds Keppel's head to her breasts in comfort. 'At least you can rest,' she sighs reassuringly. Myrtle's thick red curls drape down her back, her healthy green tail glowing like a fancy apple.

Sienna arrives next. She is on her best behaviour, even deliberately letting her fangs and claws grow out slightly to demonstrate that she has been distracted, in turmoil. *Grieving* even. Her devious mind averted from the poker-straight lines she likes to live her life inside.

And Carmine with the candyfloss hair and marshmallow-sweet heart topples in last.

'I'm sorry, I'm sorry, I'm late, I'm sorry!' she squeaks, darting about like a bumblebee that doesn't know which puddle of pollen to settle itself upon.

Bingo serves Myrtle's honeycomb, sliced, with sea-hibiscus tea, and Zar is kind to them all, proudly showing off Kai, and the talk of his resolution engages the council. Kai reddens and beams in delight and pride. The council seems small to him. He had imagined a bigger group. But when talk of the throne begins Kai knows to go upstairs with his seal pups – but he also knows he will go to a window where he is able to peer down on his father, holding court, stroking his beard, being a selfless giant.

'I've decided to step down from my throne,' he announces.

'Zar, no!' Carmine gasps. 'You are king.'

'Yes, but not a very good one.' He almost cracks a smile as he turns to Keppel for support. 'I've barely managed to look after my own family, let alone protect the Whirl. After losing Lorali I now need to focus on what's important: little Kai, my mind and, of course, my mate.'

Keppel folds herself into Zar, as though somebody has woken her from a dream after all this time.

'Your Majesty, I really don't think that's a –' *Of course Sienna has to protest; it seems more convincing that way.*

'Drop the act, Sienna, we all know I'm not up to it. After Kai's resolution I will step down as king officially.' The relief

166

of the words gives him great freedom. Sienna finds it hard to keep a smile in. 'You will make a wonderful queen,' Zar offers.

Greedy Sienna, be careful, with your crystal eyes and sharp claws. Be careful not to stumble over your swelling dark thoughts. Be careful not to stumble.

'Who said anything about *Sienna* being queen?' Myrtle throws a spanner in the works. Sienna wants to punch that fat whale right in the face but she thinks quickly.

'I was just about to nominate you, Myrtle.' *Clever, clever – try to throw the scent off your ambition. But you still reek.*

'Don't be ridiculous. I cannot be paralysed by authority. Heavy the head and all that, and I think my lower half is heavy enough!' she jokes. 'Carmine, have you an interest in the throne?'

Carmine doesn't have to speak. One wince and shake of her head, like politely trying to refuse a canapé at a formal event.

'Very well. Let us cast a vote.' *Here we go.* 'Quite simply, a show of hands for Sienna in position of the throne. If you do not agree then keep your hand down and we will think of an alternative solution.'

Zar and Keppel raise their hands, wanting the title to be taken from them as swiftly as possible. Carmine can't help but shudder at the thought.

'Very well.' Myrtle gives a smile that soothes everyone, even though it is clear she is not best pleased with the decision. *They urgently need some more council members. Sienna as queen? They may as well hand the role to the monster Nevermind.*

Sienna is finding it really hard not to cackle in celebratory evilness. Her nostrils flaring at the stench of success is proving too difficult to stop. But Myrtle isn't giving in that easily.

'However,' Myrtle adds, 'given the circumstances, after our many moons of hardship, and your reputation – no offence, Sienna – I think it best if we, the council, nominate you but the vote goes to the Mer public.'

SMUG BITCH! Sienna thinks, but nods, even managing a smile – but it is the sort of smile a shark might give a Walker before it tears its head off.

Anyway ... Sienna has anticipated this development, which is why she has taken Tip Murray under her wing. The folk of Tippi adore Murray and if Murray loves Sienna, well ... they'll surely think she is a hero. A true leader.

'I agree,' Carmine adds. 'Perhaps after Kai resolves we could cast a vote.'

'Indeed.' Keppel nods. 'Let the projections decide; the spirits will be high.'

'Lovely,' Myrtle agrees. 'No voice speaks louder than the colours of a resolution. No clearer a day to see the future.'

'Very well,' Sienna lisps. *She has to bring out her trump card now.* 'Which reminds me ... I have a salvage to resolve myself.'

The council spin around, shocked.

'You do?'

'I do.'

'But we had no idea! Is this recent?'

'A while. A long while. I guess I was nervous.' *Sneaky thing; keep on lying.* 'I wanted to keep it to myself – you know me; I like to ponder on these things before I pursue them. Besides, my maternal side was never the strongest. The salvage was so instant, and he was so vulnerable ...'

'Ah! It's a male!' Carmine shrieked, clapping. 'Even better!'

Sienna blushes. 'I couldn't just leave this withered boy – I acted before I thought.' She bites her lip. *Be careful, Sienna, you nearly let yourself show.* 'I've named him Victor.'

'Why, how wonderful!' Myrtle is chuffed for her. 'Of course this will make your campaign for the throne very appealing. As you know, to resolve is a power that shows nurturing, and selflessness. The public will warm to you. Well done.'

Sienna knew this. Which is why she said it.

'We should resolve Kai and Victor on the same day!' Carmine jumps excitedly.

'That will be perfect.' Zar hugs Keppel's shoulders. 'Bind us all back together – what a celebration that will be.'

'The making of two boys; the passing of a title,' Carmine squeals. 'I'm sure the boys will get on famously!'

Sienna feigns excitement, even though every time she smiles she feels as though she hears the ghostly grave song of Lorali echoing off the garden flowers and crawling into her ears.

'So it is.' Myrtle claps.

'So it is.' Sienna mimics the same clap, but it is out of rhythm and completely out of time.

AURABEL

IRON LUNGS

I've never tried to bring anybody back from the dead before. Unless you count myself, I guess.

I don't even know where to begin. The only thing I have is metal. An abundance of it. And my strength. I have to be strong. See her just like I see a ray I have to gut, although I'm not gonna eat her afterwards. Ha ha. No. Ah. *What the hell am I doing?*

Rummaging through my trusty scrapheap I find pipes, an old funnel thing and this pump-like device with a little tube thing at the end. I take whatever screws and bolts I can find.

And then I don't think about it. I just cut. Slicing so carefully on the marked lines down the centre of her chest.

I carve quick. A flash of red immediately appears and I regret this instantly. Still, I think I'd more regret not trying. What is the worst that can happen? She is already dead, isn't she?

And then I begin. Plumbing away at Lorali's chest. It feels wrong. Cos she is a Mer but not just any Mer. Raw red on my fingertips and it's so slippery and soft, like I've ripped open a pillowcase and released a thousand red feathers into the sea. And the metal is so old and cold and dirty next to her pure warmth. I have to work quick, quivering collapsed lungs in my palm, juddering like jellyfish.

I fix the piping up, using the tubes – like a throat, I guess. I can make the pipes work pretty easy but it's about making it look decent too. I mean, the girl's gonna have to live with this in her chest. I want to be delicate; this isn't a rough job. But I need something that can expand and deflate – everything seems either too strong or too delicate . . .

Think, Aurabel. Think.

And then it comes to me. The puppets – the four-piece band! The one with the squeezy box in his arms! It is perfect; it goes in and out, bubbles always pump out of it – surely it can act as lungs? I feel bad taking away the poor little guy's instrument, but the band will just have to carry on without him . . . or break up.

Sod it.

It's a perfect fit. I won't know if it works or not until I get the air moving inside of it but it looks the part.

It'd be ugly to ruin her skin with tacky rope. But I do have my net of hair. All woven together. We don't need much of it. Just a few delicate strands so it doesn't leave a big scar. I begin to sew. Seeing less and less of the industrial clamping I've created. Burying the factory inside her. Metal against her blood and flesh feels sore and harsh. Misplaced. Like seeing shark teeth in the mouth of a goldfish.

Like how I must look. A mess of skin and metal.

171

But I begin to feel better once I start seeing her skin lacing back together, hiding the hollowing of ribs. Hooking her back as one. Knitting together all my blue hair – *my* hair in princess skin. Seems too mad to be true. I hope she likes it.

See though . . . I was half expecting her to just wake up, you know? Just like that. But her blue, blotchy body just seems so dull and numb still. Can't see her ever breathing in and out again anytime soon. *Talking. Seeing. Swimming.* Doing all her princessy things. I feel crazy now. Like some nutty doctor, hacking up bodies and left with some sad soul on an operating table who I couldn't save.

But no, I'm not done yet. We've got these two red glove things that are attached to metal arms that go in and out. Gloves. For fighting, maybe? They come away easy because the metal is all rusty and worn down. I fix the boxing arms to the big wheel machine but with a smaller wheel lying flat. OK, now I need a . . . I rummage through all our scrap metal. I need a cone to go over her nose and mouth. Once I find a piece of malleable metal, I bend it, like a beak. It takes a while to get it right. All this cranking and bolting and it needs to be tight to work properly. Otherwise the air will get lost.

I think about me. Learning to swim again. Learning to start again – that's how I know to not give up. That's how I know that anything is possible. Even saving a life. Because I saved my own.

Once the beak is affixed to her face and the punching gloves are above her chest, I say to the sleeping princess, 'Wish me luck.' And I climb the rungs of the big wheel, the carts filled with water, and begin turning like always, scooping and plopping

172

up water. Pulling and sucking. I turn and turn and turn. And it begins to happen. The wheel is spinning the smaller wheel, powering the punching red gloves like a mill, pounding on her chest, energy raining on her heart. Meanwhile, the funnel using the air from the turning is chugging up all the fuel from the motoring action and throwing it down into her throat. The gust of air. The air she needs. I keep turning, trying not to get too excited. Her body whips as the gloves smash her ribs. I'm using all my strength, hoisting my bulky industrial tapestry of metal with me, my fingers and wrists gripping as I move robotically. Rung after rung. Her chest rising and falling.

And then – *BOOM!*

Her eyes open. They are even more beautiful in real, up-close life.

Oh my fucking cod. She's alive. I only went and did it. Lorali's alive.

PART III

Lorali

BLUE THREAD

NO. NOT BACK HERE. I –

Howl. *What is this metal over my face?* Try to lift my head, my body.

But too heavy. Beating. Punching my ribs and chest. Pound. Smash. And RAAAAAAAAHHHHH. RIPPING. PAIN. BLINDING. HAS MY BODY BEEN TORN INTO TWO HALVES? Blood. Hurts to – What *is* this metal that covers my face? The sea. Salt. Everywhere. Water. Gasp. Choke. My eyes. AGH. Throb. NO. Breathe. Panic. Heart. Thrash. No. *WHY DID I COME BACK?* Remember . . . can't you? Brain freeze. I have a . . . where are my legs?

WHERE ARE MY LEGS?

MY FEET? I have a – wait.

A tail. Tapestry.

Blackout.

I'm going to . . . My back. Stabbing pain. Eeeeeeeeesh. Flooding back. It comes. It all . . . In a second I realise. Rory! I splash up.

'RORY!'

I shout but the noise is contained. I throw this tight metal cone off my face – what is it? *Get it off.* Pressure. Worse now. 'I have to get to him!' I roar. Fight. My voice. Muffled. Not mine again. I've been captured. Stolen. No.

Who is this?

She speaks:

'At first I wasn't sure if it even was you, but I've seen you a couple of times before you . . . you know . . . and the painting in the palace . . . Sorry if I'm talking a lot. I do that when I'm nervous.' She breathes. 'I'm just so happy to see you.' She pushes me down. With the shaved head and the big eyes, she is strong. 'You can't get up just yet, 'kay?'

'Where am I? Please? Please,' I beg. I shake. 'I need to get up to him.'

How do you know me? Does everybody know me?

'I know you wanna get on but you are too weak. Your breath is connected to this wheel for now.'

NO! NO! IDIOT. NO! THE WHEEL? ISN'T THAT A WHEEL FROM A FLIPPING FUNFAIR? NO! These Mer. How ignorant they are. Just like how I used to be. I'd forgotten how backwards we all are down here.

'This is NOT a hospital!' I roar. 'This is a big wheel . . . This is a ride, *ridiculous* . . . a fairground ride!' She doesn't understand. 'It's not . . . Where is Rory? Listen to me – do you know a boy named R—' He won't have the same name any more, will he? I can't . . .

Blank. Cold. OUT. Darkness.

I sleep but in this closed quiet I can hear her talking. Shuffling. The metal goes back over my face. Nostrils closed. Mouth shut up. I close my eyes. I dream. I am too tired. Too . . .

The grunting. Punches whack my chest again. Grunting mechanical tremor. Judders through my body. Quiver. Alert. Alive again. Like clockwork. I hear grinding in my chest. It's easy to breathe again but the pain is still there. *Eugh*. Thumping. Be calm. Be calm.

The Mer with the shaved head swims back down to me.

'There you are.' She smiles. 'I know this is scary and it looks like I don't know what I'm doing. That's because I kind of don't. But you don't have to worry, about nothing. I know this is a bit . . . make it up as you go along. I get that. But I think I've got this under control. If you can trust me. Which I know is hard in a place like this. You can't really trust anybody. Sleep if you need to and I'm just gonna focus on keeping you alive.'

'Keeping me alive?'

'Yeah – you were as dead as a doornail when I found you. Why on earth would you come back down here? Nutter! Look, I fixed you, with metal, see, like my tail.'

She shows me this metal tail. I've never seen anything like it. It's a perfect tail shape but gunpowder-grey, metal, silver. Rusted, worn patches of gold and iron, copper and amber. Even coloured, in places, from where the aluminium has been taken from Coca-Cola cans, beer cans. When you look closely you can see all the minute details – cranks and bolts, bottle caps, tools – keeping the mechanics of it working. Each piece so perfectly connected they move like chain mail. Like a real tail.

'It's metal, see –' she beams proudly – 'just like your lungs . . .'

Lungs?

I lift my hand and the weight is enormous. NO. Pain is

179

screaming through my veins. I feel scabs on my arms and bleeding from my head from my fall. And I trickle my fingers softly down my front. I feel it done up like a seam. Like a hem of a dress in Iris's shop. A zip. And it answers the pain.

The wound is sore. It smarts. It dawns on me – I'm never going to be able to breathe again. Not on my own, unassisted, out of water.

'I don't want you getting up yet, but when you've recovered and can breathe without assistance, the world is yours again, princess.' She seems so happy to see me; why is she so – 'Don't cry, don't cry.' She holds me. 'You don't have to cry.' She puts her hand on me. It's rough. She adds, 'This here is my blue net. It's made from my hair – it's what stitched you back together, so it shouldn't scar too bad. The body is a miracle, really.'

THE SEA

AUTUMN

It is in Cheryl's hair that I sit, carried in the bashing breeze. Or lined on the ball of her eye, lacing her lashes. Sometimes she can taste me, wet on her cracked lips; I seep onto her tongue. She crunches over my frosting moisture on the bend of every fallen dried amber leaf; I mist up car windows and eat at brick walls, whistling in through keyholes and the missing tiles on roofs. The sea air lives everywhere and knows all the secrets.

She raps on the door of Iris Spy. It is closed because the old man is sick, again. Coughing in his bedroom, a plastic yellow bucket takes it all. The smell is bad. His legs are bloated. Puffed out and purple, all shiny. Cheryl won't see this yet though.

Flynn answers after Cheryl knocks again.

'You all right, Cheryl? Sorry, Granddad is having a bad one today. I haven't answered the door – you know what Mr Manflu is like,' he jokes, but he is in denial about the sickness, pretending it isn't eating Iris from the inside out. 'And he won't see a doctor, which isn't helping.'

'Maybe we should just take him anyway.'

'Yeah, I'll have to kill him myself first to get him there.' Awkward laughter, the way laughter is when it's about something that is true. Something that is inevitable. Death happens so suddenly sometimes; even though you have your whole life to prepare for it, no one ever really does. Never really can.

'Is Lorali with you?' Cheryl asks, the sound of my waves breaking behind her.

'No. I've been so busy here with Granddad we haven't opened up shop. Is she OK?'

'I'm worried she's gone to those stupid swimming lessons again or that she's tried swimming on her own and something might've . . . I'm sure she's fine.'

Flynn knows the swimming lessons don't exist. He didn't know what she got up to, but it certainly wasn't swimming. Her hair never smelt of chlorine.

'Yes, I'm sure she is fine. Let me know if you don't hear anything later.'

'Will do. Do you need help with your granddad?'

'We're good, thanks. He would hate for you to see him like this!' He nods. 'I'm sure he'll be fine.'

But Flynn isn't sure of anything. How could he be?

THE SEA

PIN

Murray perches nervously, awkwardly, on the wooden swing inside the Sabre Tower. Backwards, forwards, she swings like a pretty caged canary. Sienna floats up towards her with spiked walrus milk in a glass. The clunk of the chain around her wrist clanks as they cheers. Sienna wears black lace over her tail, her colours carefully concealed.

'How is the pain?' Sienna asks Murray, reaching her palm to stroke Murray's cheek.

'Still hurts; still miss her.'

'Of course you do.' She kisses her forehead. 'Take a sip of this, it might take a little off.'

Murray sips the milk. Her bones tingle.

Sienna snakes behind Murray, her breath tickling up her spine. Murray's tapestry flourishes, with jellyfish-like rounds marking her like she has been scalded by a burning pan. Sienna, also an expert at reading the marks of a tapestry, nods knowingly.

'I just wish she would come home.' Gentle tears sweep the young Mer's face.

Sienna nods, brushing her weeping away, her fingertips walking Murray's arms, spidered in sparkly intricate tattoos. Hairs on end. Sienna strokes Murray's face with her sharp claws, but it is a gentle touch, scarily soft. Murray's heart begins to stir; she is feeling something. Deep. Sienna comes close, up to her mouth, to her ear, cheek to cheek. Tension. A hot bite. It feels like Sienna is either going to suck the tongue out of Murray's mouth or strangle her. Murray can't help but feel her spine arch back. Her insides are on the boil.

'I have a gift for you.' Sienna pulls out a pin. A silver tooth-shaped brooch. 'It's my special handmade pin. It represents my home, my family. You are one of mine, Murray. You are welcome, always.'

And the fear of the sensation she was almost about to give in to evaporates.

A *pin?*

Murray has never had a family before. Never felt like she belonged to anybody except Aurabel. And she can't help but feel honoured. Starry-eyed, she hugs Sienna close. Chest to chest. And without thinking a moment longer, unhinges the prick of her Murray name badge and replaces it with the glistening pin of Sienna. It sparkles, beautifully, nearly as much as the way Victor sees her.

AURABEL

LORALI

'Here, eat this.'

'Thanks. I'm starving.' She takes the root and slither of ray.

'Good. I hate Mer that don't eat.' I watch her chew. She has tiny hands. And gorgeous round cheeks, way prettier in real life. 'How's your breathing?'

'Fine. My chest just hurts,' her voice crackles and she winces as she swallows, holding her front. She looks about as she chews. 'You live in a fairground.'

'I dunno what this place is,' I say back. 'At first I was so scared of it all – never seen anything like it – but now I know it's decent. Wouldn't change a thing about it.'

'Where are you from?'

'Tippi.'

'Ah, I love Tippi.'

'Have you been before?'

'Yes, of course! I mean, I wasn't meant to, but I'd always sneak out and visit.'

'Don't take this the wrong way, but I didn't think the royals ever visited Tippi.'

'Most of them don't. But I always did. It's an amazing place.'

'Yeah, it is pretty amazing.' I try not to get upset. She is all right, this one. For a princess anyway. Lorali gets up. I can see her ribs hurt as she swims about.

'Course this is an old-fashioned funfair. Looks years old. But you should see them when they are turned on, full with people on a Saturday.' Lorali looks glum for a moment. 'Children happily screaming, arms in the air, lights, music, the smell of sugar. Popcorn. Candyfloss! It's like a *real* treat for a Walker to come to a place like this.' She smiles.

'That's funny – I thought it was a torture chamber when I first landed here.'

'Ha ha. I would've thought that too.' She ducks under the coves and arches, lined with rocks and weeds. 'Now it all looks so vacant.' She doesn't want to offend me. 'Not scary vacant. Just different: peaceful.' Her fingers stroke her stitches. My hair embroidered around her heart.

'Hey, if you don't like the blue, I'm sure we can find something else.'

'No, it's perfect. Why would I ever want anything different?' She gulps. 'Your hair saved my life!' She smiles. 'Aurabel, *you* saved my life, and when it's safe enough for me to get back to the palace, I'll make sure you're rewarded. Properly.'

I think about my job at the palace. My responsibility. This isn't the first time the palace has promised me a reward. The chances of one are slim. But I don't care – things are different now.

'Nah, I don't need no reward, Princess.' I rub my shaved head. I actually like it without the hair – makes me feel strong, less to care about. Plus, I can move faster without all that hair dragging me down.

'I'm on the hunt,' I add.

'The hunt?' she asks, turning to face me. 'What do you mean?'

'To get who did this to me. To kill who took my tapestry.'

'I thought monsters did this to you. Wasn't it an accident?'

'They did.' I hold my throat. I don't think she'll like hearing who I am after. Sienna is in the council; she is basically royalty. 'But it wasn't an accident.'

'Aurabel! If it wasn't an accident, who is to blame?' I can see she cares; she is hurt for me. Wants justice, even. I don't know why she cares so much. I feel the anger slipping out. My darkness leaking from me, cancelling out everything. But I can't answer.

Lorali puts her hand out and strokes my head. Her palm rests on it; it feels like it's always been there. 'Whatever you need to do.' She smiles.

'We should get you back on the wheel,' I change the subject.

Lorali is able to fix herself to the cone. It looks uncomfortable but I don't help her – I want her to know that I'm not holding her here, that she's free to leave whenever she chooses. I start to climb the wheel, making the mill turn. I clamber up, mounting the spokes. I can feel her eyes on me. She is frowning, almost. It's not angry. It feels more like she's asking me why: *Why would I do this for her?* I avert my eyes and focus on the turning, sweating and pulling my arms and yanking, the metal tail beneath me weighing like concrete.

187

'AURABEL!' she shouts up through the racket of the water sloshing. 'Aurabel!'

'Oi! No!' I swim down. 'Don't take the cone off! Put it back over your mouth or else it won't work.' But she doesn't listen. And what am I gonna tell a princess?

'Aurabel, what happened to me wasn't an accident either.'

I drift down to her as she sits up.

'OK?' I come close, swimming to her now.

'Somebody wanted me dead. They tricked me, made me feel it was safe to come home, and then they watched me – they watched me die.'

'Lorali, that's horrible. What, and they did nothing at all? Why didn't they help you?' I shake my head in horror; who could just watch an innocent Mer lose their life in front of them like that and do nothing? Hmm . . . I can think of somebody who might. 'Do you know who it was? Did you recognise them?'

Lorali nods, although I can tell it hurts her heart. Her face crinkles up; it's the first time I've seen her so full of hate. 'Oh yeah. It was Sienna,' she spits. 'Sienna.'

My body sinks. I look at the industrial bulk attached to me. My dead nerves. And then up at the princess. 'Looks like we have something else in common.' I push my tongue into my mouth and Lorali says nothing. Which is exactly what we have to do: nothing. Absolutely nothing. For now.

THE SEA

HEADHUNTED

A wet wipe smeared in brown make-up. Shapes frowning, like an inkblot test of yet another day of wearing a fake smile. Speak to the mirror, Opal Zeal.

She picks at the last few remaining salty chips on her plate of room service and orders another glass of rosé to be brought up. No, make it a bottle. She isn't sleeping. That queen-sized bed is overrated. Legs are overrated if she is honest. She can't even use the stupid things. She is still *just* as paralysed. Just as reliant. Just less special. *Where is that wine?* Where is Marco?

Her phone pings. Marco. Finally.

TO: MissZeal@theworldofzeal.com
FROM: MarcoAscott@wildyoungthingspr.com

Dear Opal, my glamorous baby,

You will always be my number one wild princess. I'm SO sorry to do this over email but it was too too too too hard face to face.

I wanted to wait until the opening of GUSH (and your amazing reveal was out of the way!).

As you know I've taken on Leslie Glass, who I was doing odd bits for whilst she was here in the UK for her arena tours . . . and GUESS WHAT? She's offered me a full-time position!

Opal, I've been headhunted, by LESLIE GLASS!

LESLIE BLOODY GLASS! My all-time dream . . . I know you'll be happy for me. 'My Head Is a Spaceship' is such a banger – we always loved that tune, didn't we? I've told her all about you! She says you have the best wardrobe in the world! She's a fan! You two should do drinks!

I'm sure you'll come join us on the road for a sing-song! Oh my god, Leslie would love that. But as you know this is really and truly my dream job. Seeing the world and travelling and I've always wanted to work in music.

    I can recommend some new names for
you of assistants and publicists if
you still think you need someone,
although it seems to me that you're
not doing much at the moment. Perhaps
you need a holiday or should take some
well-deserved chill time?

    Anyway, love you so much.
    Your friend,
    Marco x

Opal throws her phone at the mirror. It cracks into diamonds
that fall on the marble bathroom floor. That's seven years bad
luck she could really do without.

    Perhaps they were right and opal is an unlucky stone after all.

THE SEA

TIPPI

Damp, dilapidated town. Easy to turn your back on the sliding dregs as they bleed and fold into one another like pages of a soggy diary. Tippi was a sour, wet, cold hole. A ditch. A dive. Visiting there, with the common Mer, was just too much effort. Too much reflection. Too much of, *It's not fair that they live like this*. But *now* they come to Tippi. Sienna has a plan. She wants Murray and Victor to sell her as queen first, get some momentum going, and then she'll reveal herself again, reward them with a visit.

Murray knows the way, of course. Sienna's serpents swirl around, not too far out, securing the young Tippi Mer and her unresolved companion.

'So this is where you live?' Victor asks, swimming behind. His tail is still an eggy off-white; it will remain so until his resolution when his colours will flood and texturise his tapestry into deep, detailed illustrations. But for now he remains neutral. No identity. Giving away no scent. Giving away no secrets.

'Uh-huh. Yep.' Murray leads Victor through, her long hair butterflying before him. He likes Murray. She is the reason for the water bubbles in his stomach sometimes. But he is professional. Polite. Happy to be the newbie being chaperoned around.

Here it is. A mangled mash of city life. Civilians living in battered shacks stacked high and spread tall. This isn't because space is limited but because they believe there is safety in numbers and prefer to build close and tight. The structures are impressive. Stacks of fallen unwanted items from Walkers or the borrowed earnings from the sea: lost boats that stole lives with them, crashed cars, coaches, ambulances. Units. Sheds. Tanks. Trains. Cars. Ambulances. Phone boxes. All piled up. A mixture of findings from all over the world. Once a piece of something drifted away, who knew where it would end up?

'This is great!' Victor soaks up the buzzing town. It is so much more alive than the Sabre Tower, which stands like a frozen, neglected cathedral. A place where it is always winter. Tippi is bright. Electric. Moves at speed. Bursting with a frenzied purr. The minute Victor stops to admire something it has vanished. There is so much to see. So much to be amazed by.

'Do you really think so?' Murray laughs. 'I reckon the Sabre Tower is much more amazing; you're so lucky to live there.'

'Really?'

'Yeah, it's so . . . *decadent*. Is that the right word?'

'I prefer it here. It's not as dark . . . it feels real happy.'

Murray hasn't felt happy without Aurabel for a long time. Nowhere feels *happy* to her any more.

'If I'm being honest, I always thought it was a dump myself.'

'Well, it's not. It's got character. It's got purpose.' Victor nods to show he stands by his statement. Murray can't help but be charmed by Victor, trying to be all official, and his sweet compliments. The lanky thing. *How'd he even end up here?* She can't imagine him as a Walker. Living. Breathing. What bad thing happened to him to be salvaged? Did he drown? Was he murdered? Did he sink in a ship? *Or do a suicide?*

Murray can't help but laugh at all the female Mer staring at Victor. New, fresh flesh. A male. She can hear their starved growls.

'What you got there then, Muz?' one shouts.

'Leave off, Verella. Look, he's wearing Sienna's tooth pin.' Her eyes glint. 'He's untouchable!'

'So is she. Look! That's new. Oooooo! Murray's wearing Sienna's pin too! Oh, you fancy now?'

'Oh, stop being a bunch of little squids!' another spits back. 'Poor thing has lost her mate, so let her do her job.'

'Thanks, Chelsea.' Murray winks.

Victor quite likes the attention. These females are *creatures*. He will *not* be forgetting them anytime soon.

A few little Merbies dot about. Chasing and playing and splashing. Young Mer are rare. They tend not to be salvaged because they remain the age of their salvation and often the hardship of the water is too much for small souls. Besides, the scent of a new child is not always potent enough to call a Mer to salvage, their traits not developed entirely, but occasionally the odd child can be saved. Like these three here. They go to Murray when they see her, holding her tapestry, branching their hands into her fingers. They have questions. Rumours have travelled.

'Murray, Murray, my mother told me you've been to the palace. Have you been to the palace?'

'No, no, only the gates, like you.' Murray smiles, ushering them along. 'Nothing special.'

'Oh.' One looks disappointed. 'But wait, what about the tower? Have you been to the Sabre Tower?'

'Yes, yes, the tower – did you go there? Are there dragons and monsters and Sienna with the fangy teeth and the claws? Is she a witch?' another adds, eyes alight, but Murray is quick to blow out their infant flames.

'Can we do questions later? We have work to do.'

'Did you say the *Sabre Tower*? I *live* in the *Sabre Tower*!' Victor grins, ignoring Murray's suggestion of questions later. He says the words *Sabre* and *Tower* as dramatically as he possibly can. Murray throws him a look.

'OH WOW!' they say. 'You LIVE there? What's it like?'

'Well . . .' Victor crouches to their level, spanning his arms as theatrically as he can. 'The walls are made of the darkest, rarest stone, with ceilings of pyrite so it twinkles, even in the dead of night. The corridors are winding and dark and you have to be *very, very, very* brave to go down them.'

The Merbies squeal hysterically. 'What about the monsters? Will they eat you all up if you're bad like Aurabel?'

Murray drifts ahead, a lump in her throat. 'That's enough.' She floats away from the group. 'Come on, Victor. We have work to do.'

Victor feels guilt swim up inside of him. He winks at the little Merbies. 'No, of course not. And besides, these monsters didn't eat Aurabel. The monsters at Sabre Tower don't eat *anybody* – they are our friends. They would never eat you guys.'

'Even the big one?'

'*Even* the big one. Nevermind cannot escape, anyway. Even if she wanted to eat you up she couldn't!'

'Phew,' one sighs.

'Unless . . .' Victor says in a very deep voice. 'Sometimes I like to gobble up Merbies . . . especially if they laugh when they are tickled!' Victor tickles the Merbies frantically; they shriek and laugh in joy. 'I'll see you soon – I've got lots of *boring work* to do.'

The Merbies all exhale a disappointed sigh.

Victor catches up with Murray. 'How cute are they?'

'I see you've made friends already.'

'That's my job,' Victor says. His tone sounds as though he's defending himself but he can see Murray seems sad. 'Don't cry. You're not crying, are you? I won't be able to see a tear*drop* in the ocean in these *current* surroundings . . .' Victor elbows Murray. '*Cur-rent* surroundings . . . Actually that's two jokes in one there, kind of . . . I'll just shut up.' He laughs awkwardly. 'But if you are going to cry, let it be over my bad jokes.'

Murray manages to let out a smile. *Maybe this Victor is OK after all.*

The meeting is being held in Tippi Hall. (A fallen aeroplane, I believe. I know these aeroplane things well. They avoid me like the plague but alas, some do end up in my belly.)

Inside, both Murray and Victor, with Sienna's silver pinned proudly to their chests, speak to locals about the advantages of having Sienna in power. They have both been briefed by Sienna. '*Play* on my weaknesses,' she advised. 'Expose my flaws before they can.'

On and on they reassure the Tips that Sienna is 'just like them' but it is Victor who has the lines on point: 'Yes, of course she was standoffish because she was isolated herself, never understood, never valued . . . a bit like the citizens of Tippi.'

They lap it up: 'Yes, she does have a temper because she is passionate about the protection and survival of her species, but the decision lies in your hands – who would you rather runs the waters? A shrimp or a shark? I think I know who I would vote for come the election.'

Murray watches Victor with the Tips, so kind and natural. So charming and endearing – he empathises, he laughs when they do, he tells stories and enchants them with his quirks and obscurely slanted nature. He sells Sienna to the Mer of Tippi, not realising that none of them want to buy into Sienna – they want to buy into *him*.

With the Tips cheering after them, Murray and Victor leave the sunken plane with a smile. It has been a long but successful day.

'Well, that was impressive.' Murray beams. 'You did well.'

'Oh . . . I'm sorry . . . was that a compliment, Murray?' Victor jokes sarcastically.

'Don't push it!'

'So come on then, which one of these strange objects do you live in then?'

'Me?'

'Yeah.'

'You don't want to see where I live.'

'Let me be the judge of that,' Victor pushes.

'No, really, I don't want to.'

'That's not fair. You know where I live. Come on.'

'You live in a mansion palace in the Whirl, Victor. It's hardly the same.'

'Come on.'

'I don't want to. OK?' Murray shouts and swims ahead.

'You don't have to – I'm sorry. I should never have asked,' says Victor as he reaches her. 'I'm an idiot.'

Murray doesn't want to make eye contact. Her heart is yearning, broken still. Eventually she looks up at him. 'Come, I won't show you my crate – it's crap. But I'll show you something else.'

Aurabel's slam lies, as always, upturned. It is covered in some trinkets and treasures, tokens that the Tips have left for Aurabel in her memory. Murray jams the door open with the knack only she and Aurabel know and leads Victor inside.

'Is this Aurabel's?'

'*Was*. Yeah.'

'It's beautiful.' Victor is in awe.

They shouldn't really be in Aurabel's slam. Tips will talk – they probably already are – but it is the closest she can get. Murray misses her terribly; she is riddled with the disease of loss. Still, nobody has said a word to her; they know what Murray and Aurabel meant to each other. And Murray loves moving about her space. Keeping the deathly shell of it warm. The idea of Aurabel's slam becoming cold and vacant makes her want to die. So here she comes. Doing things as she would.

Breathing the slam alive. Course, nobody has to know that she still sleeps on the back seat of the upturned car, or in the engine, curled up like a grey reel of cotton, clinging on in the desperate hope of not unravelling.

The photographs and images on the walls of things he has never seen fascinate him; Sienna never shows him stuff like this. 'What are all these things?'

'Walker things.'

'Walker things?'

He knows nothing. This innocent soul.

'I'm sorry I snapped at you.' Murray apologises. 'I just think Aurabel should be doing this. Not me. She was the political one. She was into all *this*. You should have seen her. She was constantly asking questions, forever speaking for those who couldn't. She was a force. You would have loved her.'

'She sounds cool.'

'She was. She was the coolest thing I ever knew.'

Murray holds her chest. Warms herself with the wrap of her own arms. Victor stands by her, not too close but close enough to feel her buzz; he wants to touch her but he knows he can't. He knows she looks at him like a child. But he doesn't feel a child. He feels that he knows more than they think.

'You know what we're doing here is making a difference,' he says firmly, with kindness. 'Sienna is going to be queen and it is down to us to spread her good word, her need for change. It's up to us, Murray, for Aurabel. To get the law in order, to get some justice for Aurabel.'

Murray shakes with sadness. 'I know, I know. I just miss her, that's all. She was my . . . everything.'

Victor nods in understanding. He knows Murray loved Aurabel with more than affection. She loved Aurabel with a rage.

'Use this anger, Murray. Use this anger to help Sienna win this election. Then we get to really punish the beasts who did this to your Aurabel. If anybody has your back, it's Sienna.'

AURABEL

WALKERS

Lorali is still laughing. 'I'm sorry, I just can't believe you thought nutcrackers were toenail cutters. How *big* do you think toes are?'

'I dunno!'

'You've seen pictures though?'

'Yeah but I didn't know, did I?' I laugh too. 'We don't get *nuts* down here. Murray also thought that microwaves were TVs and that the images were played out from models inside.'

Lorali laughs again. 'I did too! Actually, I still don't know how TV works – it's so weird up there. Though, Aurabel, nobody really knows – I bet you that most of them have no idea how the images get on the screen like that.'

'It's so futuristic.'

'I know. They never ask questions. They believe what they are told.'

'What do they watch on the TV?'

'The news – like, what's going on in the world – movies, TV shows, cartoons.'

'What's a cartoon?'

'OK . . . erm . . . You know the illustrations in the petrified forest?'

'Uh-huh.'

'Imagine those but not so abstract. Like, to look like us . . . then some amazing technology makes them *move*. They become animated. They are fun because it's playful. Kids love them.'

I love listening to Lorali's Walker stories. We used to pick Opal's brains like this but she never lived as a Walker like Lorali has. It's so interesting. I reach for another packet of strawberry shoelaces, which I just find so funny. Shoelaces? Ha! What IS this stuff? Not only do these Walkers tie their shoelaces with this red stuff, they eat it too! At least I think so. They taste absolutely delicious.

'They are much better when they aren't stale. And wet.'

Lorali's crazy – they are amazing; so sweet and chewy. I'd been avoiding the things like poison until I knew what they were.

'Anyway . . . what else?'

'OK. What else? OK, they watch this TV programme, yeah?'

'Yeah?'

'Where the show is basically just humans living inside a house. Live.'

'What do you mean?'

'Well, that's just it. That's it. Humans watching other humans, being alive.'

'Do they suffer?'

'Not really, just exist.'

'What?' I crack up. 'That sounds *brilliant*!'

'I know! It is! Flynn hates it but I love it! It's so interesting, watching them all living and breathing and fighting and laughing.'

'I bet.'

I watch her look down at her tail. She looks at it with hate. Like she wishes she could chop it off and get the legs back. I look at my tail and how I owe everything to it.

'What's Flynn like?'

'He's great. So sweet. And kind. Gentle. He does absolutely everything for everybody. He's smart. He watches all the nature programmes, and reads books. He's a great cook. You'd love him, I know you would.' She rubs her eye. 'Since Iris got sick he's become even kinder somehow – even more protective, even more understanding, more patient.' She looks out into the land of machine. We are sitting at the top of the wheel, the sea level and calm. 'He's become like a brother to me. You know, when I lost Rory I thought my body would just give up and stop working. That I'd never know how to love again, maybe even *like* anybody again. Not just that I couldn't go through the pain of losing again, but also that I wouldn't know how to do it.'

'I used to think that too,' I say. I want to tell Lorali how grateful I am that I met her. How thankful I am that she imploded into my life the way she did. But I can't find the words. Anyway, I don't think I even have to; I think she already knows.

Lorali swims away and begins picking roots out of the ground to eat. If it wasn't for Lorali, I don't know what I'd be doing right now. I owe her so much. She ain't how I expected.

Dunno – thought she'd be more superficial, being royalty and that. *And* having the experience of being a Walker for all this time. Joke of it is, she thinks she's so normal. But rah, no, wow – she's a marvel. She is a lighthouse to me. Some big shining bright alive thing that keeps me going. And I bet you anything she thinks I am the one keeping her alive. Mad, innit?

THE SEA

JUMPING THE GUN

Sienna watches Victor's mouth move as he says the words 'they love you'. *They love* me, she thinks. *They* love me. They *love* me.

'Oh, Victor, you've done so well.' She reaches for the bottle of chilled walrus milk. 'Shall we have one to celebrate?'

'I think we better.' Victor giggles as he tilts his glass at an angle. The sticky thick whiteness fills his glass as their eyes meet. '*Queen*,' he adds.

'I wonder if I'll *ever* get used to that word.' She sips the heady liquid cloud. It burns her throat and chases her nerves away, gives her the guts to inch a little closer to the young, handsome thing. His long arms and crowing neck. His dimples. His hands. Strong. Would it be wrong to –

'Murray's great, isn't she?' Victor fractures the moment with the splutter of Murray. *Great, not HER again. That is all I need.*

'For a poor Tip,' Sienna spits. 'She has issues though. She has a screw loose.'

Victor doesn't react. He doesn't agree with Sienna but he knows better than to protest. Sienna likes hearing only her own thoughts. Anything else is a nuisance. And it is rare to get her in a good mood. Victor sniffs the milk before slurping; it tastes cold and creamy, rushing with the smack of tingles feeding up and down him in shoots.

'Let's talk about *you*.' Sienna's fangs glint. 'My boy. My salvage.'

'OK . . .'

'You're going to resolve on the same day as Kai.'

'Who is Kai?'

'The king's boy.'

'King for now, you mean,' he says, knowing she likes this sort of joke.

'Well – yes.' She giggles. 'Zar's boy. They are hoping for it to be a joyful occasion – a celebration, a coming together.'

'That's fine.' Victor looks into his glass. 'I've never met Kai.'

'No, you wouldn't. Zar keeps him locked away in the palace. I mean, you can understand, after losing a daughter and all.' Sienna gulps her drink, her neck swallowing, the white cream on her lips. 'Are you happy? Do you want to be resolved?' Her finger circles the rim of the glass.

'Of course. It would be a great honour to be accepted. To be complete.' Victor inches away in his seat; he can feel Sienna dwarfing him. He says the words she wants to hear. 'To be yours. Officially.'

My ocean can almost hear Sienna's voice crack. 'You will never be mine.' She looks at him. 'When you are resolved you will be free. Liberated. Completely – to swim . . . to explore . . . to *tessellate*.'

Victor looks nervous. He's heard this word knocking about in conversation but never learnt its true meaning.

'Do you know what that word means, Victor? *Tessellate?*' She spreads the word out long and strong like a back rub.

Victor shrugs. Shakes his head. He gulps his walrus milk. It goes straight to his head. Red chest. Red cheeks. Big pupils. Spilling. HOT. HOT. BLOOD. HOT. Sienna tops up his glass.

'I'm sure you can imagine . . .'

'I –' Victor starts before Sienna pushes the glass of liquor up to Victor's lips with her hand, holding the bottom of the glass with the scoop of her hand, like she is feeding a baby with a bottle. Whilst Victor drinks Sienna corners him again, thrusting her tight body into his.

'It was just an idea, of course . . . but I've been thinking . . . I don't want you to embarrass yourself when the time comes. It would be nice, wouldn't it? To get some *experience* before you meet somebody new . . .'

Victor feels the heat of Sienna arresting him. She takes a clawed hand and begins forking her fingers over his skull like a rake. 'Soon I'll be queen; I'll be very busy. You can have anybody you want. You will be a prince.'

Victor, lost for words, looks down, drinking for something to do, but only getting lighter with each sip.

'Don't you want to learn?' her split serpent tongue rattles.

And then Sienna leans forward, eyes closed, hands rough. She pounces on Victor, breathing deep. Her tongue weaselling down his throat. Her scales trying to lock into his, trying to fuse and merge them together. The moment so fast. And intense. But he can't. He doesn't want to.

'I'm sorry.' He wriggles out from beneath her snatching vice. 'I can't. I'm sorry,' he pants, his hair a mess. And Sienna flushes violet. Immediately, collecting herself up, undoing every action she just did, reversing her feelings of attraction towards him and replacing them with venom.

'It's that Tippi bitch, isn't it? You love her, don't you?'

Victor stays quiet. Says nothing.

Sienna sinks her drink, wipes her nose. 'Don't you?' she roars. Her humiliation spitting feathers. Victor knows better than to reply.

Sienna shrugs, pretending not to be hurt. Sucking herself up, zipping her feelings in.

'Well, she doesn't love you,' she spews. 'Aurabel was not her *friend*. You know that, don't you? That *Aurabel* –' she says her name as though it is a joke – 'was not her friend at all. She was her *mate*.'

Her spite does not stab. Victor, seeing Sienna in a new light, just observes as she crumbles. Barricades himself from her viciousness. But his silence revs her up another notch. 'She doesn't want *you*. You don't have the *body* for it. You are weak. You are tiny. You are not a *she*.'

And Sienna storms out of the room, drunkenly bashing into the stone walls. A bruise. To mark the moment she punished herself.

Lorali

LITTLE CREATURES

'There you go.' I release the lobster out of my hands now that Aurabel has fixed her up; she looks stronger than ever with her new metal body parts. More scorpion. A flicking hinged tail that is made of the mini loops of a bicycle chain, forks for pincers, the edge of a nutcracker/toenail clipper for a claw. This is how we pass the time. Saving the glorious freaks whose bodies have fallen apart or stopped working. Taking a break for my breathing.

I've learnt now that we are all creatures and can outlive our bodies through our minds and souls; bodies can get tired, break and let us down, just like machines. We slow down, we stop, but that doesn't make us dead.

It was a joint decision to wait. To bide our time. I wanted to plan my return and not just bulldoze my way into the palace. Sienna had wanted me dead, enough to drag me down here, just like she wanted Aurabel dead. And there must have been a reason for that – no matter how tough I find that pill to swallow, it is the truth. But first I have to find Rory.

Besides, I am still regaining my strength. Although my breathing has recovered, I still can't go for more than a couple of hours without fixing onto the mill wheel to pump more air into my lungs. And even when I feel fit and strong and full of breath, ready to fight my way back to the palace, I know that the performance of my breath is hidden in that giant metal hoop shadowing over me. It is like Iris's inhaler for his asthma, constantly topping me up. It won't be too long until I can go without it completely.

Aurabel and I reach the top of the Big Dipper. I swim and Aurabel climbs. Everything has to be a challenge for Aurabel. The rusty clanking runners scream as she hauls a cart up to the top and we sit inside the carriage waiting for a break in the water to send us sleighing towards the ground. We try to float like spacemen but inevitably sink like bricks from our metal organs. But we hold hands. Eyes closed. Drifting in the weirdness of our belonging in this strange environment, to this even stranger friendship. This union. I am angry at how sheltered the Whirl is; how it treats Tips with its monstrous class divide. The friendship I've found inside Aurabel is more genuine and equal than any of the relationships I've found in the Whirl before. She is my friend. My real friend. A girl. Who likes me rather than laughs at me on the street.

Endless days of laughter and joy in the fallen fairground are healing. We revolve and worm our way around the industrial scraps. There is always something new to explore or invent. We eat sea-sap and drink ourselves numb on the heady toxic sugar syrup of the old canned drinks from the vending machines – the gas has flattened, and the film coats our teeth like sludge and makes us dizzy. We swap and dance and roll and talk and smile until we wear ourselves out, and then sleep under the canopy of fairy moss, in the clutch of a broken trampoline. Spread out like a starfish in the House of Fun, catching coloured balls from a ball pool as they bob away like particles of a polka-dot rainbow.

It is peaceful. Making happiness from sadness, our will to fix what is broken, in every sense. Aurabel trains and trains; even in the water I see the sweat drip. And I breathe in and out. I'm learning to breathe all over again. There is so much freedom for us, because of course this heavy life of rusty metal and bone is a struggle but it is an afterlife. A hideout. Because everybody thinks we are dead whilst we are *so* far from death.

We are immortal.

THE SEA

FLYNN

At the kitchen table. Flynn waits.

Sent home from the hospital to get some rest.

He doesn't know if he's waiting to be told that his granddad has died.

Or if he's waiting for Lorali to burst through the door like always:

Eyes glinting, cheeky smile on her face, coins in her hand . . . to send him to the bakery to pick up cake.

But the doorknob doesn't twist. His phone doesn't ring. And sleep seems like it will never come again.

THE SEA

VICTOR AND THE TIPS

'Well, *obviously* it's a moon counter!' Victor grins as he stands by the grandfather clock in the centre of Tippi Square. 'Do you see the hands? Every time it goes dark and we see the moon we can flick the little hand round to the right. Each mark scores a moon . . . When the big hand is all the way back at twelve again it will mean that twelve moons have passed and we can mark the occasion.'

'Yes! With a party?' one of the Merbies suggests.

'Well, why not? Now we have a concept of time here in Tippi we can party right through from one moon to the next!' he jokes, and the Mer giggle.

'It's genius!' an older, gruffer Mer shouts out, pinning her hair into a mound.

'He's the genius! Can't *he* be queen?' another adds.

'We all know what happened the *last* time we put a male in charge!'

'Now, now, folks! Come on. Zar has done his best,' he

sbrushes them off gently. 'I'm happy just to be here with the Tips.'

'Who's gonna move the hands on this bloody moon clock then?'

'Good point.' Victor stands, hand on hip. He is a handsome thing now that he has grown into himself: chiselled jawline, groomed brows, his tapestry slinky yet strong, almost feminine. The Tips take in one another. It will be a big responsibility . . . who is responsible and dedicated enough to be in charge of the clock?

'Can't you do it, Victor?' a Merby asks, unsure how the question will go down with the others. Murray laughs. Victor is quite the favourite here, slotting into the town of Tippi as though he has always belonged, quite like the moon itself. Aurabel would've liked him.

'Yes, Victor. Come on, you can do it!' Murray claps. 'It has to be you.'

And before Victor knows it the Tips are chanting his name and he is trying to calm them down, but it is no use, it is decided. He can't help but blush, the way he always does. That same shade of pink he goes whenever Murray looks his way. She is everything the night before was not. He wants to escape the sickening trap of that memory. Caught in the deathly web of a black widow with a taste for fresh meat. He just has to keep his head down and continue with the campaign; Sienna said it herself – once she is queen, she will be occupied. And that couldn't come too soon.

I pick up speed for the serpent-pulled chariot. On the ride back from Tippi to the Whirl the pair pass the fields. Wild

214

herbs, tangles of mangled shrubbery and dusty pom-pom heads shaking in the currents. Murray has an idea.

'Have you ever tried seaweed before?'

'Errr. I think you'll find it's pretty much a staple ingredient in the diet of any underwater specimen,' Victor replies cheekily.

'No, *smoking* it.'

At the peak of the Dreng, a dip in my break, the two sit before the emptiness, puffing seaweed, with a view of the overgrown field, home to jellyfish. Swanning in and out like carrier bags, like boneless umbrellas. The serpents, still chained to the chariot, graze on greenery and plump morsels buried deep in the chalky bed. Grateful for a break.

Victor passes the seaweed back to Murray; she takes a toke and breathes acidic green apple haze into my quarters.

'Do you think things will be different after your resolution?'

'Not really. I mean, I'm looking forward to having more independence . . . but I always feel like I've been myself.'

'Do you think you'll still come back to Tippi?'

'What do you mean, Murray? Of course I'll come back. I love it there.'

'OK. Good.'

Victor repositions himself. Leaning on his elbow, he scratches the back of his neck. Fiddles with some grassy knot screwed into the mound beneath them.

'I've been meaning to ask you . . . on the morning of the resolution, do you think you could come to the tower? Sienna says there is a parade . . . I would love for you to be by my side – you know, only if you want to. At the white rock.'

Murray is taken aback. It is a big ask. Mer only have their family and mates by their side at the rock . . . For Victor to ask her to come to the tower in the morning would mean them arriving together. That she is unified.

Does she want that? What would Aurabel think? What would the Tips think about her and Victor? They would assume something is going on between them . . . so soon after Aurabel too. But what was this sting between her and Victor? Should she ignore it? She knows she feels something towards him . . . Is she stupid not to join the Whirl? Be loved, protected, powerful? She can't decide if Aurabel would be proud of her for surviving . . . or disgusted. Backstabbed, even.

'Wow, don't seem too eager.' Victor elbows Murray in the ribs sarcastically. 'You don't have to, really. I just thought you might want to.'

'Sorry. Yes. I would. I would love that. I do want to, but I just . . .'

'But?'

'I don't have anything to wear,' she jokes to soften the tension. 'You need to have the best outfit in the whole Whirl to be up at the rock like that. You've seen how I dress; it's hardly the –'

'Murray. Shut up. Please. It should be everybody else worried about how they'll look next to *you*! They all need to up their game!'

'I look weird.'

'You've got character. It's nice. I like it.'

'OK. OK. I want to come with you.' Her eyes light up like planets. Victor smiles. He can't help it; he wants to hold her.

'Sure?'

'Absolutely.'

'That's made me so happy.'

He thinks about touching her now, but no. He feels the warmth in his hands would burn her with his obvious desperation. He plays it cool, takes a toke instead. His cheekbones draw in, his brows coming together in concentration as he inhales.

'I can't believe I'm sharing my resolution with someone I've never even met before.' Green smoke teases out with his words. 'Who even is this Kai?'

'I met him once – only briefly.'

'Did he seem OK?'

'Yeah. As nice as you can be for a *prince*.'

'Watch it!' Victor jokes. 'I'll have you know that could be me one day!'

'Oh apologies, Your Majesty!' Murray laughs. 'Mad that both of you have the chance of being royalty.'

'Nah. Don't say that.'

Victor passes the seaweed back; she takes it. Murray's hair softly fans through my ripples. Her tapestry shows flowering blooming hoops; dilating psychedelic pupils. She touches her pin from Sienna.

'I don't want you to feel trapped in any way.'

'I don't feel trapped, Victor.'

'Good. I know . . . But Sienna . . . she can be quite overpowering. I want you to do whatever you want to do.'

'I am doing what I want to do.'

Are you? Are you doing what you want to do, Murray? Let's find out.

217

Murray's heart stutters awake. Victor holds her gently, trying not to show too much in case she steals herself away. The result of the inevitable, irresistible electric fuse crackling between them is both of their lips locking together in sweet seam. So, for now, it's innocence bound inside the mutual niceness, the raw natural simplicity of when you just really actually like somebody, and they just really actually like you back. *That* makes a good kiss. *That* makes a really good kiss.

But Murray feels the peering eyes of Sienna's serpents glaring at them. Guilt prising its way into the gaps. She sobers from the moment.

'I can't,' she says. 'I'm sorry. I like you. I just can't . . .' She breaks away, stealing herself from the shot. Leaving Victor to dull in the fading, muted frame.

But he grabs her hand.

'Don't be sorry,' he says. 'You don't have anything to be sorry for.' He too feels the drilling eyes of the serpents; their escort back to the Whirl comes with eyes and ears and judgement. 'Come on, let's get back, Sienna will be worried about us.' Murray nods and he prisons her eyes inside his. 'Everything is going to be OK.' He clenches his jaw. 'I promise.'

AURABEL

HUNTING

'That's it.' Lorali throws a handful of multicoloured soggy rice grains to the ground. 'I can't eat these bloody Rainbow Drops any more. I need some *real* food.'

I do too but I don't feel quite ready to leave the funfair. I have become used to snacking on bits here and there. But I know I am just avoiding the outside water. I've really softened since I met Lorali and I have to keep my grit about me. Can't lose my intention now. But it is hard not to like Lorali. Hard to keep to my regime when I'd rather just sit and while away the day with her. All her stories of what life was like as a Walker blow my mind; it never gets boring. Hearing about the people, the animals, the air, the temperature, nature – and course I have so many questions about cars. I knew I was right about roads. She told me all about this Rory and when he first found her and the lighthouse and the smoking huts. The good bits and the bad bits too. And I even told her about my mate, Murray, a bit. And that is rare for me as I don't like to talk about things that are too close to my heart. I always used to worry that every time you speak about something that is precious to you with somebody else, you are giving away a bit of that preciousness. And I never wanted to share Murray with anybody. Now I have no choice.

'Helloooooooooo? Are we going then?'

Lorali is right. We need a feed. We need real meat. Can't be doing with nibbling on this fish food when I am training, and now we have to split and share it.

'All right.' I talk myself into it. 'It will give me a chance to *finally* test out my net again.' I gather up my recycled hair and bunch it under my arm.

'Gosh it looks heavy! I didn't realise how big it was.'

'My hair was all the way down there. It's a LOT of hair.'

'Must've taken you ages to make.'

It did. I was so excited to finish it. I've been waiting for ages to use it, so why am I now putting it off?

'I can't imagine you with long hair.' She smiles. 'Or *any* hair, for that matter.' I feel stronger with her around me; she buffers the loud, scary voice in my head, behaves as a constant tonic that keeps me in neutral.

I look back at our adventure land. Seeing our little fixtures and inventions to make life easier, our beds made out of the stretched canopy of marquee tents and trampoline skin where we sleep side by side. Why do I feel like I never want to leave?

Suddenly I have my doubts.

The water is rushing and dipping all on its own. I have a wary, terrible feeling in my guts that today isn't the right time, like something bad is going to happen. I try to anchor myself.

'It's quite foggy; why don't we go out tomorrow instead?'

'We can't live on just rays and strawberry laces for ever, Aurabel. We're only going to the edge to practise using the net. We're only going to catch a fish and then we'll come back.'

''K.' I nod but I feel unsure. I feel limp and a bit sick.

'You don't have to be afraid,' she tells me. 'I'm here, OK? You're not on your own; nothing is going to hurt you.'

She takes my hand and we swim towards the edge, away from the metal world, away from what I know.

'Just remember, we can't be gone long. We don't know how long you can be away from the wheel before you need a reboot,' I remind her, hoping she will change her mind, but she keeps swimming ahead.

'I'm like an old rusty machine!'

'Oi! Don't you knock old rusty machines!' I joke.

'It's true!' she giggles. 'I'm completely reliant on them now! Who'd have thought I'd need a fairground to keep me alive!'

'Neither of us ever really liked the easy route though, did we?'

'No, I suppose not.'

We swim out, further and further, where the water is colder, thick and almost white.

'Gosh! The water really *is* foggy!' Lorali admits and we curl through the current.

'Told you!'

'All right, it's my fault, sorry.'

'Don't suffer! I'm glad to be out – I was the one being a shy hermit crab.' I feel more in my comfort zone reassuring her than her reassuring me. Still, I don't feel any better about the whole thing.

'Sing it again . . .' I ask as my tail cranks and parts the water – I am proud that it swims so smoothly. Lorali's organs drum along musically next to me, her chest thumping with its jagged heartbeat. We sound so loud out in the open, away from our machine friends. *Bash. Bosh. Bish.*

'The same song *again?*' she asks. And I nod. I love hearing Walker music, so different to ours. She sings this light, delicate song that's so happy and human and tender. So comforting. I want to sing along but even though I can imagine how to make the sound, my mouth can't do it. Anyway, it calms my nerves listening to her sing . . .

My eyes, in the density, start to naturally search for fish. My confidence grows. Game-face on. I feel so pleased to be out in the streaming corridors of the ocean again, thrashing my way around. And just when things couldn't get any better I see some kill. Beasts that'd be fit for a meal – no, wait . . .

I know those beasts, don't I? And my heart begins to squeeze.

Loralí

AURABEL'S NET

'Bastards!' she roars and, before I know it, she's gone. Whipping away, following the rush of steady ripples pattering behind the cluster of rocks. She must have seen a good hunt. Dinner.

'AURABEL!' I shout after her. 'Aurabel! Wait!' I scoop and duck after her but she's going so fast and the water is so murky it's hard to see.

I follow the silver spark of her tail. A shooting star. Weaving and scooting, buzzing in and out, and as I get closer I see the wisps of the turquoise hairnet, blending in with the curves of ocean. I whip my tail up quicker as the push of Aurabel's heavy tail thrusts against me like a tidal wave; giant folds of water flush towards me, kicking and shoving me back, making it hard to catch up. I push again, harder, like the water is a wall, and engine myself to a steady speed. I see the frothing of bubbles and can make her out, charging ahead, close now, Aurabel, aggressively tearing through her own choppy current, hunter head, gritted teeth, growl, net, sharp blade of a knife in her left hand.

Then I see the beasts. Sea serpents. Long eels. Stretched toads. Hissing swirls with clenched jaws stuffed with dagger-like twisted teeth that split the mouth like the thorns of a rose.

She wants them.

But I see they are not alone. They are not free creatures. No, they are connected to black ropes. And I realise whose serpents they are.

Sienna's. *That's* why she wants them. I want them too . . . just not like this. Not yet.

'AURABEL!' I roar, almost angry this time. This wasn't the plan. But it's too late; she is already bundling them up into her net made of hair. Her tail whipping up the sand into a storm, foggy; I can't see through the billions of grey particles.

AURABEL

REVENGE

So fucking angry I don't see a thing. Nothing except the acid raw blind rage of revenge steaming through me, blowing down my bloody veins I'm so angry. I'm gonna catch these fucking beasts so fucking quick. Got them off guard – basically asleep on the job, these creatures. I dig my knife into their throats, not enough to kill them but to threaten them, to make the steal real nice and easy. I hear Aurabel scream for me, even in the rough of it. I know it wasn't part of the plan but I've got to concentrate on not slashing the faces of these beasts that have haunted me every day and night. I might never get this moment again and I'm not gonna lose that. I'm not gonna cheat myself the way life cheated me. The way it cheated Lorali. But there's grit everywhere, dots of sand and fog all whizzing in my eyes and mouth, hard to see through the greyness of it. Still, I'm too mad to care. I feel the tug. The beasts aren't alone.

And then I make out the black ropes of the chariot. *Fucking great*, this is it. This is it. NOW! COME ON! COME ON,

SIENNA! Lorali is still shouting my name but I'm deaf to her now. I know it's not how it was meant to be but just give me that wicked witch; let me kill her.

But it's not Sienna steering.

It's a male. A . . . male . . . and no, that's not Sienna neither. Not the council member of the Whirl . . . No, that's my . . .

It's Murray.

In Sienna's chariot. Wearing Sienna's fucking pin. SIENNA'S FUCKING PIN. Where's her Murray badge gone? Where's her . . . And I lose sight. I can't. I shrink away. I am weak. I dwindle into soup. I don't want her to see my hard metal tail. My bald head. My ugliness. My bleakness. Pathetic. Small. I hide my face. Turn away. So they can't see me. But it's too late. I'm sure they've seen me.

I shrink. Too wasteful and weak to see my girl. For all that strength I had. For all that work I did. The weakest fucking muscle of all lives inside my chest, wasting away like a diseased liver. I am gutted. Backstabbed. The monsters, the serpents, slip free. My net opens like a blue flower and then spills apart in tears, lets go like a waterfall into the endless bounds, and the chariot darts away.

Lorali

SAVING A HERO

I know my breathing is slowing. As I stop to catch what murmur of breath I have, I hear my sore lungs beating for me but the sound patters away like footsteps running in the distance. My body is thundering with fear. Rioting inside, I feel vulnerable and lost in the density of this place I don't know any more.

Aurabel.

I feel so weak. Delirious. Like I have been spinning around to Iris's records, tripping and spinning. Sick and weary. My head feather-light as I dip and dunk and I . . . see Aurabel, sinking, losing herself and her net, a rain of blue strands melting away like an aspirin in water. I gulp in the misery. Take her body over mine.

She is limp, her eyes closed in sadness. 'No, leave me,' she says, 'leave me here.' She is drunk on the blueness of it all. Her eyes dull and faded. Her edge, now just crumbling debris.

'What happened? Aurabel? Who was that? Tell me, what happened?'

But she doesn't answer me, only collapses into my open arms. She's heavy. Like a hero. I realise how much more I care about Aurabel than I do about destroying Sienna.

'I've got you,' I whisper as my chest crackles, like it has water in it, a foggy sound that swallows. 'I'm not leaving you anywhere.' My lungs stagger, fighting for air, collapsing, like I've got the world sitting on my front. But I won't let that show, not to Aurabel. And with my last remaining strength I do what I know I can do: take Aurabel home. Back to our rusty home, where even the little fire of our spirit seems to have been blown out in one small ironic breath.

'Murray,' she whimpers. 'That was Murray.'

THE SEA

THE MYSTERIOUS MALE

'Who *did* this?' Sienna booms, her voice rattling off the walls of the Sabre Tower, her serpents on her lap, sore heads sulking on her hips as she strokes them. 'Do you know why I named you Victor? It's for *victory*. Did these idiots think they could kill you? *MY boy? Before* your resolution? HA! Fat chance!' She shakes her head, jolting walrus milk in her bony hand.

Murray and Victor sit side by side on the stone wall in her drawing room, glaring at the yellow-eyed beasts. *Do they know their secret? That they kissed? Will they tell?* No. Both know Sienna wouldn't like it. *Why is that so?*

'Mer. I mean, this is the sort of work I expect of monsters, sure – Walkers, even – but not Mer! Who would do such a thing? And you're sure they saw the black ropes? They knew you were in *my* chariot?'

Victor nods. 'We think so.'

'Did you not even get a look at them? Can you not remember anything?'

'Just the one Mer – a male. But only from behind. Shaved head and muscly, strong. He wore armour.'

'Armour?' Sienna racks her brain.

'Yes, his tapestry was hidden in a shield,' Murray adds.

'He could be anybody!' Sienna snaps.

So Murray did not recognise her love, not without her teal hair, not with her new strength and ripe anger. Aurabel is big now, built and hard. Who was this mysterious male with the metal tail? The colours masked. Unreadable.

Sienna slits her eyes. This isn't looking good. She thought the Tips were coming round to her; they seem to adore Victor. But now *this* . . . They must've followed them home. Or some new conspiracy. Why, this is treason! She was being attacked! Somebody wanted her dead. They weren't to know she wasn't in her chariot.

Victor has begun to notice the anxiety in Sienna, when she is agitated or nervous. Grinding her teeth. Her jaw clenched tight like a knotted ball of elastic.

'It was the monsters he seemed to want,' Victor says reassuringly, not wanting to lose sight of the campaign. 'I think he was hunting. I don't think he initially knew the serpents were yours. He was angry, hungry, this Mer. I don't think he cared who the beasts belonged to.'

'In fact, he stopped attacking when he saw the serpents were attached to the chariot,' Murray adds. 'He let the beasts go!'

Sienna isn't buying it. 'Of course he wanted to kill the monsters first, because then I'd be vulnerable, without protection, and of course he stopped attacking because he didn't want to kill you . . . He wanted to kill *me*!'

Sienna isn't one to sit back and let the dust settle. No, retaliation is her forte. She has no choice but to take matters into her own hands. The beasts will be sent back, in a pack, to kill this strange hunter in his armour. Whoever he is.

Lorali

BACK ON THE WHEEL

One. Two. Bang. One. Two. Bang. The boxing arms punch my chest. Murray turns it. Not saying a word. The earth crashing on her shoulders. Her eyebrows in a frown. So that was Murray then – the Mer that left Aurabel in a spin.

One. Two. Bang. One. Two. Bang. The pain doesn't hurt. I wander in and out of sleep, dreaming. I go through every thought, every frame of mind.

One. Two. Bang. Regret that I came back here. Regret that I ever left. Blame that I'm here. Guilt for Rory. Guilt for Aurabel; my injury holds her back. That I suggested even leaving to hunt. Guilt for Cheryl, Rory's mum. Flynn. Iris. I miss my mother and father but I'm nervous to face them too.

One. Two. Bang. What if I feel as disheartened as Aurabel when I see Rory again?

I see the golden beams of sun bake the broken stars of sea shells, tickling the arms of weeds, touching the broken vehicles of our broken fairground. There's beauty in the way the sea

dances, surrounds you like a friend, supports and hears you. As though it's alive. This deep, hidden world of mystery that I once called home fascinates me still. And it crosses my mind that perhaps he is happy here. Rory might not want to ever go back to Hastings. And even if he did . . . I wouldn't be able to follow him home anyway.

THE SEA

A TAIL BETWEEN
THE LEGS

In a blacked-out Range Rover Opal sits in the back seat, rivers of
black mascara running down her cheeks. She swigs neat vodka
from a bottle. Her eyes jolt behind her Miu Miu sunglasses
with the speed of the vehicle, clicking at the passing buildings
and the way the space seems to grow when they get out of
London. She can already taste the recognisable smell of me as
they get closer to the coast. Not even the car air freshener in
the shape of a green tree can mask a familiar smell like that.

The lighthouse stands like a vase on a tablecloth, as though
you could pull the strip of pebbles out from beneath it and
risk the whole thing toppling over. There are so many things
she wants to say to Lorali. She could start with an apology.

'Do you want me to come in with you?' her security asks.

'No, no, nobody can hold my hand through this one.' She
smiles briefly. Another swig of drink. Pop an upper. A chewing

gum to hide the sour fog of booze. And in the pocket mirror, lipstick. Running her tongue along her whitened teeth. Her wheelchair won't work on the pebbles; she'll have to be carried.

Security lifts Opal to the threshold. In her fur coat she looks like shot game in the arms of a hunter. Opal leans forward and bangs on the door. *Bang. Bang. Bang.* Over and over. *Bang. Bang.* 'I'll wait.'

But she will be waiting a long time. Nobody is home. Flynn and Cheryl are sitting in a hospital waiting room, sipping coffee from plastic cups, waiting to hear if Iris's heart is still beating or not.

AURABEL

SILVER PLATTER

I woke up in a fucking rage, didn't I? I'm not sad about it. Can't be sad about it. Have to get over it, don't I? Already resigned myself to the fact that I've lost her anyway . . . *Murray*.

FUCK. Why didn't I say anything? Why did I just . . . Why now? I wasn't ready. I knew I wasn't strong. Should have listened to my instinct. I just have to train more. Do more time on the ladders, the wheel, tracks, sweat it out. Get strong.

Still my knuckles tighten as I relive the feeling of having their necks in my palms. I could bite the air. Squeeze the life out of any . . . *breathe*.

'I'm sorry, Aurabel.'

'Why you sorry? Don't be sorry.'

'I was the one who suggested we leave.'

'It was my choice, Lorali, and I'm glad I saw what I saw. I was meant to see that.'

'What does it even mean?'

'Means she's sided with that bitch.'

'She probably thinks you're dead.'

'Yeah, well, she's right. To Murray, I am. Clearly.'

But wait . . .

What was that . . . Don't tell me . . .

I tumble down, quick as I can. Got to do a couple more paces to get the momentum of my tail going. The tail starts moving on its own eventually. Can't get there quick enough. I curve down, past the 'dodgems', as Lorali calls them. Whatever they are.

Stay low.

Over to her, *quick, quick, quick. Psst. Shhh.*

I put my finger to my mouth, *shhhhh.* My heart.

Bang. Bang. I clap a hand around Lorali's mouth.

It's me. Don't wriggle. Don't scream.

I slide her body so her back is lying on top of mine, like when a Walker saves another Walker's life from water – it's how they go about it; I've seen it. She doesn't fight it. She trusts me.

I feel my line of hair in her skin. I feel her metal lungs, bulky under my arms. Her heart Frisbee-ing about inside that cage.

Keeping low, we crouch in the control box. It's where Lorali showed me a Walker would stand to make the rides go round. There are all these controls and buttons and a microphone. When we're there I whisper all quiet to her: 'Stay here. Don't come out. All right. Stay here. Do not move until I come back to get you.'

'What is it? Please don't leave me, Aurabel. I can do whatever you need to do.'

'Keep your voice down,' I bite, almost angry – but I fucking am, though not at her; that's just my demeanour these days.

I'm defensive as hell. I see her eyes look scared and I remember that she's told me how she's been left before. In the past. And that was when bad things happened. When she was left. So I grab her. I'm not emotional. That's not me. But I say it because I never ever say what I need to say and that's always how I manage to fuck everything up. I say, 'Listen you, Lorali – I know it probably isn't the same the other way around because you're a princess and that, but you . . . are actually my only friend. And at first, with all this, I had reason to kill, even if it meant killing myself too. But now –'

My voice breaks; I swallow the fear away and begin again. 'Now that I've got you, things are different. Things have changed for me. Now I want to kill but I want to be alive too. Because I want to be alive so I can still be friends with you afterwards.' I feel embarrassed so I say something to make myself look less like a wimp: 'Do I make myself clear?' I point to her and she nods.

She gets the point.

And I swim out of the control box and into the tilted sunken burial ground of adventure. Where Sienna's monsters have come back to say hello. And this time, they ain't going anywhere.

SAS – Selkie Appreciation Society

<3 <3 <3

YOOOOO!!!! MERMAIDS ARE SOOOO LAST YEAR! WE R THE FIRST EVA ORIGINAL SELKIE/SILKIE APPRECIATION SOCIETY. THS SITE IS EVEYTHNG U ND 2 NO ABT THE WONDRFUL MYTHICAL CREATURES THT R SELKIES. IF U DNT NO WOT SELKIES R THEN U PROBABLY SHUDNT B ON THS PGE AS A LOT OF THS WILL PROBS MST LIKELY GO OVER UR HEAD. BUT BASICALLY . . . PUT IT THIS WAY . . . U CUD KNOW A SELKIE. U <u>CUD</u> EVN B 1!

LetMeTakeASelkie: OMG! OMG! I think my neighbour is a Selkie. She is really hot and always wears a roll-neck polo top. What should I do?

SecretSelkie7: @LetMeTakeASelkie Why don't you ask her, politely, in private?

Zombierudeboy: @LetMeTakeASelkie Throw a beach ball at her head and see if she catches it on her nose.

MySelkieNightie: @Zombierudeboy MEGA LOLS!

SecretSelkie7: @Zombierudeboy PRICK

IMissZayn1D: How do we know if we are a Selkie?

RIP.OPAL: @IMissZayn1D If you're literally a 10/10 stunning hot ting that is sensitive and listens to opera and can cook really good and you never feel the need to trim your pubes.

THE SEA

A LITTLE TOO LATE

The sky begins to get blacker and the stinging chill clamps at bones. Fireworks smatter in the sky. Blossoming rounds of violent colours; scoring shrills that whisk up the sky and sprinkle the air with rust, fire, dust, smoky burnt ends. Opal asks her security to walk her to the sea. She wants a better view of the fireworks.

'It's freezing, Ms Zeal.'

'I can't feel it. I'm numb!' She grins, her eyes rolling in her head, and she shakes her bottle.

'Ms Zeal, if we take you to the sea we are putting you in danger. It's our job to protect you.'

'Who employs you?' Opal leaves the question hanging in the air. 'Well then, take me down to the shore, thank you very much. If you wouldn't mind getting another bottle of vodka from the boot of the car too?'

'Ms Zeal, we really don't –'

'I didn't ask you. Now you can watch me from the car if you *must*, but drive home for all I care. I want to wait here.'

* * *

Opal, head on the stones, her washed-out pink hair trawling the confetti shells. She peels off her fluffy fake eyelashes clumsily, murmuring to herself, swigging from the bottle as she wipes them off her fingers like dead bugs. As the fireworks pop and crack overhead, the colours repeat in her pupils, and she sees herself. More drink. A little song maybe. And now she faces me. Finally.

You act as though I never existed, old friend. Why the silence? Did you think you could forget me? Did you think that sitting in baths of me would be the same as it is now? Sell me at a water park to pacify your loss? That you could do without me? Burn me out with bright city lights? It never makes you as breathless as you are now, does it?

I kiss her toes. In white foam, I sprinkle and splash. I touch to show forgiveness. But she cannot feel me. They are artificial. They do not belong to her. It's like holding a doll. The legs do not work. But then she inches forward. Lets her fingers stroke me. *There we go.*

'I'm sorry,' she says. 'I failed you, Lorali. I promised to bring you home and I couldn't do that. And then you asked me for help and I couldn't do that either.' She drinks a little more. 'Because I was jealous. Because you found a life here; you made a mark. You are important and precious and loved. It is me who is nobody.'

She has no idea that Lorali is with me again. No idea at all. Silly billy.

Above me, the sprinting blitz of a firecracker, a rocket, a champagne cork blissfully letting go. Raining down bubbles of yellow-white fire. I watch Opal.

It gets me thinking about this story I am telling. About these three Mer and how they are all connected. All needing what

242

the other has. Lorali with her tail but metal lungs, Aurabel with her lungs but metal tail, and Opal . . .

Finishing the bottle, she throws the empty glass behind her shoulder, leaving a smeared hot-pink lipstick-kiss stain. It doesn't have to be this way; she is *still* a mermaid. Isn't she?

Let's find out . . .

Cold. Icy. Salt. The salt crystals sting her wounds. She winces. She is sucking seawater in, trying to make the gills pump, the air rise, so that she may breathe like she used to. But the dummy legs are weighing her down. She is suffering, struggling, and I am too rough to fight. She panics. Flapping. Up, her head bobs, then back down under again. Water down her throat. She can breathe steady but she's too fragile. She can't swim, can't move without her tail. Mannequin. Breathing now. But differently from Aurabel without the tail; she won't let herself sink to the floor. Water, swallowing, down, treading water but too heavy. Crawl, crawl, tug. She sees rock in the distance. Through my waves she drags herself like a beetle through cream. Swim. Swim. But she's petrified. They all hate her in the Whirl. Everybody hates her everywhere. Another half-baked idea in the split mind of Opal. She doesn't know what she's doing. She doesn't know who she is or where she belongs. She sort of thought Lorali could help her out with that, which is why she came. Why does she have to be out? *Living a life?* Her security are searching now. Running towards me – flapping black jackets and ties that wave like flags.

'No. *Leave me. Let me be,*' she whispers. She goes under. She can breathe nicely in me; doesn't that feel better? You don't have to try.

243

Wait. They are coming. Calling her name. She drags on the rocks beneath, where they can't see her. Long enough for them to think she's dead. Or gone back. They don't know the laws of the Mer.

Eventually she makes it to the cold stone. The land. It's wet and slimy and moss-covered. Hair drenched, mascara black tears drizzling down her cheeks. As she finally stands to balance.

Then I hit her. Hard. A little too hard, maybe. She topples. Slips. Into a cliff face. Her prosthetic legs smash, break off and sink down and away.

She scrambles for them. 'NO! MY LEGS!' she screams. She cries. She sobs. Reaches for them. I eat them up. A smacking torso. Like a barnacle, she shrinks into the wall. Clinging to the slimy rock face. Her chipped nails cracking on the grimy green wash of weeds. She uses her arms to rake herself upwards. Turtle-like, she crawls, makes it to a semi-flat surface where the wind and me mix. Pounding and smashing ice-cold drizzle against her and she cries. Her make-up washed off. Her heart rinsed out. She wrecks and riots and screams and ruins. Just like a firework. She was once, for a moment, beautiful, but now she is burnt-out ashes, somewhere hopeless between land and sea.

They always say that the opal stone, although a stone from the sea, doesn't much like going back in the water.

Lorali

WATCHING A MONSTER
KILL SOME MONSTERS

I cannot *not* look.

The landscape is silent. Still. The rides are ghostly. Desolate. Dilapidated, crumbling iron. Faded, miserable colours. In the silence I gulp. Think of Hastings. Alive on a weekend. A Saturday crowd, screaming. *Aurabel. Where are you?* What is she doing? The bright green leaves of plants sway lightly. But I fear they are dancing something deeply terrible. A school of foil fish dart away in an arrow of urgency. Something doesn't feel right.

And then I see the serpents; Sienna's. Five of them. Scaled snake-like beasts. With their claws as sharp as railings and fangs for teeth that could puncture the body of a tank. Their eyes, slicing, glowing a horrible evil. My heart falters, sinking deep inside my metal chest; Aurabel is the strongest Mer I have ever met but can she take all of these monsters down . . . *alone?*

Where are you, Aurabel? Come on . . .

I almost can't watch as the serpents pause. Twitch. Tune into their senses like they've heard a snap. *Aurabel*. And then I see her, lurking, behind the fallen arcade machine. She seems a monster herself right now. Her eyes a colour I don't recognise; they narrow and slit. She is biting her lip, like she is about to pocket a snooker ball. She lunges back, leopard-like, and out of nowhere launches herself onto the back of one of the serpents. With her strong arms she wraps herself around the neck of the thing. It hollers some hideous high-pitched groan and then gags and she grits her teeth and, using the weight of her strong body, crashes her metal tail into the two neighbouring serpents hissing behind her.

The knock blows them both to the earth as the weight of her tapestry is so heavy. Two left. Eyes on eyes. They dart towards her. One immediately rushes forward, gulps into her neck like a love bite. *AURABEL!*

Aurabel's blood swans into the water in ribbons. But she growls and spits and punches the very same serpent in the face. No. Like an *actual* punch in the *actual* face. Hastings pub-brawl fighting. The serpent wobbles and falls away. The second serpent rockets up and back down again, gushing Aurabel, throwing her body onto a metal fence. She smashes into metal spokes. The metal from her tapestry scrapes against the rusty rods. I feel the clang of the material run through my bones. My teeth grind all chalky. The impact. She groans. Her body scratches, bleeds. Her skull . . . a giant gash down the back. Spine, split. I want to help. But this is Aurabel's battle. She's got it.

Now the other serpent has come too. Both are crawling up towards her, snaking closer and closer. Their talons creeping up her bruised flesh. Their teeth glinting, snarling. *GET UP, AURABEL! GET UP!* She scrunches together her whole face and, using her tail once again, whips up, cracking the serpents under the jaw and knocking them both to the ground. She whimpers.

It is done. They're defeated. She pants, bent over. She looks at me through the glass and winks. Grins, even.

'Princess!' she shouts. 'I only went and did it, didn't I?' And she whoops and begins rallying up the dead striped lines on the ground: her trophies. 'Come on, you weaklings, come on.'

I see now that they are not dead, not one of them – she is *that* good. All are cranky, writhing worms on the floor but Aurabel is pleased. She has them as she wanted: half dead. Not to torture but to train, perhaps. She boots them with her fin, rolling them over, wrapping them up in fish wire. They are bleeding, eyes rolling, tongues lolling. Brave Aurabel, with her black eye and cut neck, her navy purpling flower bruises and breadcrumb dots of flecked, bleeding scabs. She smiles triumphantly; she is a step closer to her revenge. And I smile back. Glad to see Sienna's beasts on the ground.

But then I hear the twist of a chain. And it coils a wrenching knot in my gut. The water seems to suck back and the life within it vanishes. I feel the tremor of the bed below rattle through me . . .

And out of nowhere Aurabel is thrown far into the hoop of the Big Wheel. Smashing against the spokes, she clatters into the carriages, the sides toppling down as the whole ring collapses into the bumper rails, broken jagged edges of trail as she thumps to the ground. I watch as bubbles tingle out

of the debris. The shell of every clam seems to slam shut . . .
I can almost hear my breath slithering away . . .

She has been hit. Like a tsunami. By an unstoppable beast.

This is not just any beast of Sienna's. This is a beast that has
been sent. This is *the* mother beast, Nevermind.

THE SEA

NEVERMIND

They have all heard of Nevermind but never seen her. She lives beneath the Sabre Tower under lock and key. A prisoner by a lifeline cuffed at Sienna's wrist, wrapped around the beast's body. Too dangerous. Even as she arrives now her body is still shackled to the wall of her prison; she fights Sienna's battles, still with ball and everlasting chain. Stories of her weight and size send shivers down spines and fill Mer with fear. Her cave is known to be so dark and cold that black ice grows there, thorns of frost so robust they could burst through the fire-hot sun like a spear. Of course there are rumours that Sienna beats and whips her. Feeds her rancid ocean dregs, the rotten bones of Walkers. And when there is a storm in my waters, I hear Mer blame Nevermind – screaming, crying, bawling for her freedom. They say she crawls on all fours like a mammal, crushing everything beneath her, for she is the size of a small island. Could dwarf a cruise ship.

Nevermind is a predator. She could effortlessly swallow a phone box. Nevermind's tail alone is as dense and as heavy as a tree trunk, her palms like cars, each claw the size of a Walker. And the most fearful thing about her is that she hasn't finished growing. She is *always* growing. Gaining size. Nearly everything she touches attaches itself to her body: rubble, rubbish, anchors, brick, stone, bones. Small fish and shrimp paddle about her, like flies on a cow, as she is a constant food supply. Little bursts of shrubbery bush and brambles of weeds harvest in her side. She is a walking landscape.

And she is angry.

The legendary myth, cast off as the reason for the glacial arctic spells that starve the Whirl of warmth, is no longer in the shadows. No longer fiction. But now here, before us, charging into the funfair, she storms.

Lorali

MEETING NEVERMIND

On all fours, she staggers towards us. She lurches, like an elephant. It is impossible to see her features. To tell what belongs to her skin and what doesn't. Plucking up squashed cans of drink, vending machines, rope, bottles, rags, carrier bags. It's like the whole of Iris's shop and Hastings pier is glued to her body, everything tangled in the knotted web of junk. Her face, impossible to guess, a swamped mass of mess on this horrific giant head. An overloaded donkey, a full rubbish truck.

Where is Aurabel?

I hold my breath. Have to. My metal chest, grunting. Nevermind clambers off, sniffing, towards the rollercoaster, to find Aurabel . . .

But then she's here. At the control box. I squeal. No sound. Duck down. Back under the counter. OK. OK. OK. Breathe. Just concentrate. But thinking of Aurabel. Out there. Me. In here. No. I slip up again. My fingers curl around the edge, lifting myself up to get another look. I gently rise. I hear the breath of her. Snuffling at the box. Which seems to rise, almost wanting to cling to her body too. I feel the box lift.

In the corner of my eye.

Right at the window.

I jump. Hold.

Shaking.

Waiting . . .

And then . . .

The breath of the beast exhales at the window.

Steams up the screen. A rich, musky mask of condensation.

I gulp. Trembling.

The thickness of her tail curling up, clamping up and around the control box with a bang.

I slow my chest. I know that noise in my lung, that sound like old trainers thumping around a tumble drier.

And the beast can hear it.

I breathe slowly. Through my lips.

Close my eyes. The box rattles.

Cracking.

Each scale of the creature caresses the control box.

The junk accessorising her body decorated like the gypsy hands of a fortune teller in costume jewellery.

Bulking. Bashing. Brushing. Eerily delicate now.

Teasing.

Nevermind toys . . .

Takes her time.

Locked down for so long it's as though she wants to prolong the moment before the kill.

Make it all worthwhile.

Wrapping around me like a snake coiling around its prey . . .

Face to face.

Her nostrils snort, storm splashes of grey gunk.

My body locks.

The box begins to crush a little more.

I scream. Tongue ridged, like a newborn baby.

I can't help it. Closer. Closer. Tighter. Tighter. The walls are coming in.

And it is then that I see her eyes, deeply buried under the scrap. She is blind.

I have an advantage over Nevermind.

As the box begins to give under her weight, I rush my hand forward to the door seconds before the metal collapses around me.

Darting out into the open water, I pick up a wedge of metal. It's heavier than I expected. My wound smarts. I hover it above my head. It's heavy against the sucking of the water. I throw it as far as I can, aiming for a carriage tilted on its side. It smacks with a *ting*. But it's enough to make the blind monster's ears prick.

She prowls over to the echo of the noise, but begins to trip in the traps of the fairground. She is agitated as the metal loops and hoops grab to her, stumble her. She moans and roars. Frustrated. And I turn just in time to see Nevermind crouch backwards, up onto her hind legs. She walks like a Walker. Walloping the seabed in giant zombie strides. She is mammoth. Scooping up the ground with her stance. This time, I can't find my tongue to scream even if I wanted to, as I watch the dizzying angry fish spin into a spell.

253

I quickly dive down towards Aurabel, where I find her broken. Bleeding and cowering with her wounds.

'Aurabel!' I rush towards her, taking her in my arms. 'Come on, quick, come on – we have to leave.'

'I told you to stay in the box,' she drones. She is tired, sleepy almost. Covered in blood. Her eyebrow is split, her lips purple, bruised. Her body is damaged. She looks like a broken toy.

'I know you did. Sorry.' I don't want to tell her that the box crushed me and if I hadn't got out we would both be dead. 'Come on – we have to move! Now!' I hear the staggering pounds of Nevermind behind us. Every angle of the fairground is shaking. Aurabel's home, our home, ripped to shreds. Nevermind roars and it clamps my brain. Worse than any noise I've ever heard. I try to scoop Aurabel up but she is a deadweight.

'This is me now, Lorali. I'm too weak. I'm a coward.'

'No!' I shake my head. 'You are not weak. You are not a coward. You are the strongest Mer I know.' I try to peel her off the seabed but her tail is refusing to move.

She snorts. 'Thanks, Princess, but it ain't true. I fall to bits at every hurdle. Everything I touch turns to shit. I can't do this any more. I don't have the strength. I can't keep fighting. Leave me here, will you?' She lets the heaviness of her body slide her down so that she's on her back. Bloody. Battered. 'It's not worth it any more. Look at us.'

She is right. I feel just like she does. Tired. Hopeless. Weak. We are both the same, at the bottom of the dark, cold crack between tin, steel, metal and rock. Nature and mechanics side by side. Our bodies made of the same stuff. We have the same code. We are new sisters. Leaning on each other for survival. As the pounding paws of Nevermind stomp closer we resign to this ending. If we are to die, at least let it be on our terms. At least let it be at the hands of the biggest beast in the waters.

I hold her hand. It's limp and bloody. I grip it. Tight. Wait for the ending as the bellow of Nevermind gets nearer.

And then I see it.

I have never seen one in real life before. I've heard the myths about the luck they bring, the depths a Mer or human would swim to, just to find one. To hold it. Or sell it.

'Aurabel, look . . .'

'Princess, please. I know you're only trying to be nice and that, but don't. Just get out of here, please. Go and get your boy.'

I lift it from the sand as it sits so perfectly, like the jewellery in a box at Iris's shop. We would've put this in the glass case, it's so precious and beautiful. It's got to mean something. You don't just *find* a blood pearl relaxing on the seabed, especially not one that's made for wearing.

'It's a blood pearl!' I gasp. 'On a string.'

Aurabel suddenly turns to face me. 'You what?'

'Here, look.' I hand her the string. The ruby-red pearl dangles perfectly – this isn't one of nature's accidents. This was deliberate. Something somebody made with intention. Just like my lungs; just like Aurabel's tail.

'My cod,' she mutters. 'Murray.' She bursts into tears. Falling into me for not even a moment before strength hauls her back together as she sniffs. 'This belongs to me. I thought I'd lost it.'

'What are the chances? Must mean something.'

'Do you mind helping me get it on?'

255

'Course,' I say and she wraps the string firmly around her wrist. I help her knot it tight.

'Lorali, come.' And then she bolts back up, the groaning cry of Nevermind breaking through the waves like a titan. Aurabel cracks her knuckles.

Ready for war.

AURABEL

FINDING NEVERMIND
PARADISE

Bloody hell she's a big 'un. I can't quite take her in. All that size. That beast. Big blind thing swiping the air, growling, tumbling, falling about. The sound coming from her is blood-curdling hell. This beast is too great for me. And I'm tired too.

I have to think of something else.

Watching the lumbering monster. The world sticking to the soles of her feet, her mass. That bloody chain, weighing her down, reminding her that she is a slave. I watch her. She's a bit like me in a way. Rioting privately in the dark. We're both prisoners. The hell I live in every day. The ball and chain of my new skin. That I had to learn to love because it was the *only* way. My tail. What am I grieving for? My old life that seems so distant I can't even remember what I did, what I thought about back then. Now all I think about is freedom. I see myself in this beast. If I were chained to a wall all day, linked to a bitch like Sienna, I'd be pretty fucking pissed off too.

I'd be thinking about freedom.

And before I know it I am scrambling around the ground, trying to find whatever tools I can.

'What are you doing?'

'Looking for something to undo that bolt with.'

'Huh?'

'I'm gonna unscrew this beast. I'm gonna set Nevermind free.'

I try to ignore Lorali's shouts as she tells me to stop.

'Aurabel, she will eat us. Eat us all! She will destroy the Whirl; she'll destroy Tippi. She's on a chain for a reason! Think about Murray.'

'I am thinking about Murray – that's why I'm freeing her!'

Hands working hard, bloody and sore, and the metal of the chain is so old it's rusted, slicing into my open, gammy, gory wounds and stinging like hell. The rings of metal so stubborn, refusing to come away. 'Shit. Shit. Shit. Shit. Come on. Come on,' I curse.

But she's heard me. The metal chain, moving – she senses it. Nevermind revolves her body round to face me. She is coming closer. My hands can't turn any faster.

'Lorali, Lorali, help!' She's reluctant but joins me anyway, trusting me enough to help me work the metal, loosening a screw.

'Aurabel . . .' she snarls through gritted teeth as she begins to help me unpick the links chaining this beast. 'You're the one with the screw loose!'

Quite funny for her.

258

But the beast is snarling, growling, moving; more metal gripping onto her body. Her breath alone could rip your hair off. Lucky I don't have any!

Still, turning, turning; working the screw. Nevermind bends up, like she's about to stomp on us, barking in our faces. I feel her rancid rotting body up against me, so close I can feel the hairs of her nostrils, the warmth of her tongue, the . . . smell is . . . bleugh – *turn, turn, turn, quick, quick, quick* – and the heavy chain comes apart, crustily breaking away from its armour of caked mud, slinking to the ground.

Nevermind grunts, freezes, her whole expression releasing. Everything changes. Silence. She frowns. She steps away, backwards, footing the broken chain to see if it's real. If what she thinks has really happened is true.

'What's she reckon?' I whisper to Lorali. My head's so light I could pass out. Nevermind stops the silence with a cry. So desperate, I can't tell if it's anger or annoyance or sadness. Maybe it's fear. Sometimes captured prisoners don't want to be freed. They don't know what freedom is like.

But then she does the oddest thing. Nevermind slowly slides forward, tipping onto all fours, like a building collapsing. We leap back as she drops. Buckling onto her knees, she squats. Then she lies down. Submitting to us. She is grateful. In gratitude. She doesn't want to hurt us. She wants to disappear. She wants to be invisible.

Then, she comes up again, moaning, on all fours, crying with relief, shaking her body, heavy, hard. As the chain unravels, so do all the mounds of rubble strapped to her, peeling off from the connecting ties.

'Watch it!' I scream, and Lorali and I have to cover our heads, running and hiding as the chain peels away from her sides, objects spinning off her and firing through the water. And she pounds softly away, bits slipping off her gently as she is, at last, liberated.

PART IV

THE SEA

GATHERING SLOWLY,
OLD MOONSHINE

At Zar's palace a humble celebration is happening. It is custom, in Mer culture, that the family of the resolved should celebrate the night before a resolution, especially with royal resolutions. Usually this is a lavish spectacle of a party that invites all to rejoice and bless the new child of the waters. But the royals decided against a decadent party. A colossal banquet didn't seem appropriate with the loss of their daughter last time. And of course, with tomorrow being the day that Zar steps down from the throne, it seems a sad affair – the turn of a chapter.

Instead, watch how a small family of three quietly sip chilled watercress and smacked sea-cucumber jelly soup from giant seashells. Lobster tail and samphire salad, steaks of fish, fermented whale bread broken. Of course there are cocktails: fizzy honeysuckle from waxy palm-leaf flutes and squid-ink liquor and walrus-milk Martinis to dull the aches.

Dessert is bite-sized tiles of sea-salt fudge. A cake too, made from honey from the petrified forest (which is terribly hard to come by; Zar had to hunt for it himself) and rose-petal shrubbery. Bingo, playing butler, welcomes the guests inside the palace. Just Myrtle and Carmine, paying their respects. They bring gifts.

And just before Kai takes himself to bed he watches his tiny family in the garden from his wonderful view above. Not knowing what to say or how to be. Wanting to put his arms out and say sorry. *Sorry that she is gone and I am here.* Maybe, *Sorry that I am not her* – but really wanting to put his arms out and say, *What about me? Am I not enough for you to love?*

Nervously he prepares for tomorrow, fantasising about the Whirl outside. What he will be and who he will meet. But for now, it's just him, his thoughts and the groove of the scar on his chest. An unexplainable circular hole. One that nobody ever mentions. But, funny, nobody else seems to have one. A perfect shiny round scar like his. Just like the wounds on the fish that return home from his father's scavenger hunts.

A little way away in my shoulders, beacon moonlight glows inside the Sabre Tower. Sienna raps on the walls of her salvaged's room before entering with a smile.

'It's here.' She comes towards him. She is dressed. The china-white of her shawl clashes against the cream of her hair. 'Innocence' today. A good look when resolving a salvaged; an even better one when trying to become a queen. Her tapestry quakes a foggy mist. She looks like a rolling marble, gliding along Victor's bedroom. 'Are you ready?' she hisses softly, when Victor wants to ask the same question to her but thought it out of turn. He has not slept soundly in his room since she pressed herself on his mouth like a gag.

He stretches his arms. 'I cannot believe it.' His ripe muscles, plunging biceps. Just tight, youthful skin wrapped around warm, red natural tissue. Thumping with blood. Alive. He hides himself, plays his body down.

'It's come so quick.' Victor cricks his jaw.

Sienna nods, feasting on his chest, his hip bones poking out like the fins of sharks, heading for the pelvic muscle, thrusting into a perfect V before his tapestry begins. *Her crown will live there*. She thinks, *Let me leave that crown just there, every night, like a cushion to rest my head upon*. She plays with her ivory-coloured hair. 'Just a year ago you were in my arms and now look at you. All grown, ready for your colours, ready to be a merman.'

Victor sits up from his bed of sponge reef. Yawning. She strokes his arms. 'My handsome child.' She kisses him on the head. Her hands grope his neck like she is force-feeding him. She leaves the kiss to linger, hoping the invitation will engage them in a little more, but Victor shuffles out of her grasp. It feels wrong. He doesn't want it.

'I must get some sleep. Tomorrow's a big day, what with the vote.'

'I don't want you to worry about the vote,' Sienna feigns. 'It's *your* day tomorrow.'

'It's *our* day.' He smiles politely, not wanting to rile her. Playing nice. How strange it is that she looks so young but appears so old now. Cringing. So out of touch. Sometimes he is afraid of her; sometimes he feels sorry for her.

'It is our day. You're right.' She worms a tongue around a filed tooth. 'The resolution is also our bind. You *and* I.' She wants to lick his body. Drink it up. Snort it. 'And *not* anybody else. Just *us*.' Her gravelly voice hangs in the air like old-lady perfume. 'Don't you agree?'

'Yes, of course.' Victor nods. He feels unsettled, unsafe. Something is amiss but he lets a, 'Yes, just us,' escape from his pink lips.

The moon, a golf ball wrapped up in gold paper, falls up, takes a bow and overturns, ruffling my diamonds with yellow.

THE SEA

A GOOD DAY FOR
A GOOD DAY

Today is a good day for a good day, isn't it? A parade first;
the Mer must rejoice. The whole of the Whirl are invited to
celebrate. Mer dress up with coloured hair: blood red, coin
silver, dolphin blue, treasure gold, coral orange, sunshine yellow,
weedy green. Tattoos spiral up arms, garish designs of happiness,
freedom, union, harmony, gratitude, peace. Jewellery hangs
from belly buttons, rocks and ice studs pierce ear lobes, chains
and ropes hang from hips, and spikes made of metal and tusks
of wood jut through noses.

'I'm surprised they are even waving at us,' Zar says through
a gritted-teeth grin to Keppel.

'You are not a *terrible* merman, Zar, you're just a terrible
king.' Zar nods and even manages a smile. Truth is, the Mer feel
sorry for him after the death of Lorali. Things, perhaps, will
not be quite so bad for him in the aftermath of his leadership.

His fall from grace not quite so bumpy. Beard groomed, hair combed, he waves. Proud. If only Lorali were here. It is frowned upon to speak of the dead so he holds her in his heart, where she makes the beats play on time.

Keppel has wrapped her hair into a long plait. It reaches the bed of me, a twist of yellow golden straw, a spill of honey. The grey bags under her eyes have lifted. The redness is back in her cheeks; the missing sparkle from her eye has returned. They could have done this a lot sooner if only they had worked together. Then again, 'if only' is a bloody harpoon of a phrase that only leads to a slow dead end.

Inside the Sabre Tower, Sienna has a costume change, into a dramatic black netted veil, her neck decorated in black onyx. Black opals and diamonds shroud her fingers and wrists; so heavy with jewellery, this beady-eyed witch, that she would drown again if she were a Walker. Her cream hair is locked up, strung into a face-lifting ponytail. Her eyes are smeared charcoal-black, her cheekbones hollowed in theatrical contour. Her poison mouth is tainted a skull-like black in a heart-shaped kiss. Still, as oil-black and sticky tar-like as her tapestry is this morning, she is a strikingly attractive, ferocious force of a woman that would make the most beautiful of Walkers piss themselves with embarrassment. What can I say – it's the work of the water.

Back in Tippi, Murray is getting ready too. 'Shit.' She knocks over one of Aurabel's instruments. A small harp. Its arch crumbles away in her hands, the wood is so rotten. With Victor, feeding power to Sienna, her whole town is behind her, on her side, fighting for Aurabel . . . so why does it feel like the opposite? As though she is undoing all of Aurabel's rights? She pulled away from the kiss but she can't stop the feelings. Or the fact that it happened. And that a bit of her wanted it to. As she finishes sticking stones above her brows, she can almost hear Aurabel's musical little voice yelling at her to change the mind of the Tips. They thought they were being loyal to Aurabel by sticking Sienna on a throne, but really . . . Murray isn't quite so sure that it is loyal. Then again . . . Murray isn't even sure if she knows what loyalty is any more.

But as soon as Murray soaks up the spirit of the Whirl her tune instantly changes. Seeing her folk in delight evaporates her hunch. This is good. This is what the Whirl needs. Yes, Sienna is a force, yes, she is outspoken and fearless and tortured and, yes . . . a bit scary too – but isn't that what they need in a queen? Yes, she sees it in the faces of the Tips. That this is exactly what they need. Besides, as much as it hurts her to admit it, Aurabel isn't around any more. She doesn't have to live with guilt on her shoulders. She has to move on.

Murray snakes up to the Whirl with the others in the parade, laughing, rejoicing. Past the palace where she thinks for a moment of that odd quiet thing, Kai. She has never forgotten that day when they spoke through the palace gates. Now he will be getting ready for his big moment, nervously preparing to be exposed and realised. Maybe then he will be able to hang with Murray and Victor and the others. Maybe then he'll be able to step out of the shadow of his princess sister who he never got the chance to meet. Zar waves at them through the palace window. He throws tiny shells out as tokens of thanks.

As the parade moves on past the palace, Murray breathes

in the relief of change. She is excited to see Victor. She has thought about him a lot; she isn't exactly sure how she feels about moving forward with him yet . . . she isn't ready for that with anybody yet. Especially not a male. *Eugh!* But he makes her feel good for now. And there is nothing wrong with that. He will be waiting to see her smile from his window as he prepares for the day ahead. And she wants to be there, of course, smiling back. Blessing his resolution, blessing the tower of Sienna . . .

Oh, and about that tower of Sienna's . . .

The ground outside Sienna's tower . . . it's not a garden fit for a queen but a graveyard for a heinous villain. Hundreds of silver Selkie skins lie like rolled-up unwanted rugs, their soft skins heaped up like dead bodies in dramatic protest and theatrical, angry rebellion. Murray, staggering at the sight can only clench her teeth and try to swallow the stone of denial down her throat. The Selkies are right. Sienna would make the worst queen.

Horrified, Murray is in shock. *Has Sienna seen this?* She rings the great bell of the tower and is granted entry. She is here to accompany her friend to his resolution.

'MURRAY!' Sienna shrieks when she sees the Tip. 'How lovely of you to come.'

Has she not seen the seal skins? Is she not worried?

'I'm sure you've seen the Selkie drama outside. Mass suicide. Good riddance, I say. Can't imagine much of a life for them as Walkers. Still, some never learn.' She smiles.

But Murray does not smile back. She tastes a rancid sourness in her throat. 'Where's Victor?'

'He's getting ready, of course. If you don't mind I'd rather he doesn't see anybody before his resolution. As you know, it's a big day. I want him to stay focused on task – no distractions.'

'He asked me to come.'

'Oh, did he? Well, he should know he has to get ready.'

Murray looks disappointed, *annoyed* even. She wants to see Victor once more as he is. In case he changes. Murray wants to talk to Victor about the Selkie skins – *has he seen them? Are they just going to ignore them?*

Sienna smiles at Murray but it is false. This day is meant to be between Victor and her. Why is this Tip muscling her way in on their big moment? Three is one too many. Sienna looks Murray up and down; she can see she is sickened by the Selkie leathers. She has to fix this.

'Ah, yes, forgive my memory – I have so much going on, what with the ceremony and the campaign. Victor did tell you to come by,' she lies. 'He thought you might like to borrow something to wear for the ceremony.'

'He did?' Murray seems a little unsure; she thought Victor liked the way she dresses.

'I think he thought it would be nice if we all wore the same colours . . . Come on, don't be embarrassed. You don't have to wear Tippi rags.'

Rags? *Rags?*

But it is Victor's day; if this is what he wants. And Sienna's clothes are quite a big deal. She has the best accessories and jewellery in the Whirl. It would be pretty amazing to wear her possessions . . .

But what if it makes Murray look like one of Sienna's possessions herself?

Murray follows Sienna into her chamber. She feels as though

she is being knighted as Sienna opens up the door for her, which is usually bolted shut with an iron claw. Inside: designs and fabrics of lace, silk, satin, crushed velvet . . . beads, bangles, headdresses, veils, materials and textiles, pouring out of the open mouths of trunks and chests. Gawping shells stuffed, dripping like overly iced cakes with elaborate costumes. It is Murray's dream.

Sienna lays a shoulder wrap of stones over Murray's naked shoulders, just to break the ice, to show her that she is free to touch whatever she wants.

'Wear what you like.'

'Really?'

'*Really*.' Sienna cracks a grin. 'Stay in here all day, if you like.'

Murray is stunned, overwhelmed; she's never seen such beautiful findings, ever.

'I'll tell you what – I'll go and finish getting Victor ready and you find something to wear.'

Murray likes the sound of that. She immediately feels better. Sienna is so misunderstood; all the Mer have to do is get used to her.

And Murray is left in the chamber of the soon-to-be queen to play dress-up.

As Murray rummages through the accessories, she wraps in borrowed beads and netting, rope and twining, icicles and jewels. Pins and clasps. Capes and shawls. In Sienna's many mirrors, Murray can't help but steal a squeal of excitement as she catches a glimpse of herself, as *someone*. Dressing, changing, thinking of Victor resolving and what could be. *What can she wear for him? What will he think of her?* The more she dresses, the more she realises how much she does actually care what Victor thinks about her. She needs to look wonderful. Just like Sienna. But there is so much to choose from, every colour and fabric . . . the ruffled cuff sleeves and drapes and finger-loop wings . . .

And what is this . . .? Something catches her eye . . . This most dazzling, beautiful thing from the back of a trunk, shining, pink, blue, illuminating, almost smiling at Murray from the deep . . . It reminds her of something; she feels an affection towards it, like she's seen it before, like she has admired it from afar . . . but more than that, maybe . . . more like it belonged to her? As she reaches down to touch it she knows as soon as her fingers meet the fabric, immediately, that this is not fabric.

This is a tapestry.

It is slashed with scars, sewn up like patchwork. Still twinkling in a sad, faded way, like the eyes of an old lady.

This is no ordinary tapestry.

This is Aurabel's.

And Murray screams, dizzily, is sick, vomiting up a brown bitter slop. She runs to the door to tell Victor. To shout. No. DON'T. DON'T TRUST HER. So sick and angry. So enraged and confused and she has to get out . . .

But the iron claw is bolted shut; of course it is. Sienna could not help herself – she has a war to win and the last thing she needs is some stupid Tip messing things up.

THE SEA

A JOINT RESOLUTION

It is calm. Two young boys meeting for the first time.

Victor, a shrewd, striking beanpole of a Mer; long arms, long neck, natural grace.

And Kai. Dark haired. Light eyes that challenge my own for drowning pools with their wonder. Broader shoulders but still slight. The silver-hooped scar shimmers like fish skin.

These boys, even for their youth, have *lived*. Have stories to tell. And as I wind back, knowing who they are, I can almost taste what is important to them. Sniff them out as the hungry dogs they are. For these are not just any two boys. These boys are strong, resilient, full of heart and alive. Not dead at all, but thriving young men, given a second chance, and I know why they were salvaged and saved. For their valiance.

Over the white rock in the centre of the Whirl, the pair steal nervous glances at each other. Eyes on each other. Sizing up their strengths. Their weaknesses. Examining the obscurity of it all. The fuss.

Red hearts beat as the boys lie on their altars. Bodies bound in chrysalis wraps made from seaweed, they shiver with nerves under the open tilt of my surface. Sienna stands at the head of her salvaged.

'Where's Murray?' Victor asks Sienna.

'I'm sure she'll be in the crowd somewhere. Forget about her for now.'

'Did she not come for me?'

Was the kiss too much? Has she not forgiven him? Does she not want to know him any more?

'No. Sorry, were you expecting her?'

'Yes – she will come, she said she would come . . . Can we not wait for her?'

'No, we can't wait, Victor. Not for anybody. Least of all for some dizzy dank Tip who you've got a crush on. Get over it.'

Rage fizzes through the young Mer's blood. He is really starting to hate Sienna. He can't wait to get this thing out of the way so he can leave.

With the resolver behind her, the empty rock lies before them, ready to paint the language of Victor's tapestry. And Kai, moments away, but kept so far, the protective king behind him. Keppel at his side.

On balconies above sit strings of Mer. Present for the double resolution but also for the turning of the crown, the vote that is to happen after the resolution itself. This is not just a resolution of any two Mer; one of these boys will be prince by morning.

Blessed oysters, drunk from the scoop of their shells, swallowed by the boys, then both Zar and Sienna wet the salvaged ones' heads in kissed water. The resolver allows the projections to commence. Never the same are these murals. All is quiet as the colours splatter, mutate, spasm, dance.

Kai . . . We see his kindness, his heart, his strength, his curiosity, his loyalty, his love for nature, his sense of humour, his bravery. He is liked, valued. This humble tail is full of charm. Decorative, considered designs are now transferring onto the scales of his tail. An impressive tapestry.

Now the king is proud, so grateful he retrieved this lonely falling star from my hands. And that shows here too: a Lorali-shaped shadow features. Of course, Lorali was their child before Kai, so perhaps this illusion is the foreboding shadow of her slipping away and him arriving . . . But no . . . here she reappears again. It is *her*, unmistakably.

Keppel rubs her stomach; her faded stitches seem to unpick, carving a hideous gash into her pelvis. She must hold on. Keep control. Find the strength. She is saddened to learn how much of Lorali has interrupted Kai's projections; guilty, even. She has gone. But still here; the dancing Mer casts shades across Kai's tapestry, skipping now with legs and painting pictures so vivid it seems as if their daughter has resurrected, bursting through the walls and home.

Kai's memories . . . have they been triggered too? As the strange, pretty girl with the bewitching grace springs across his history like some spirit fairy conjured up by voodoo magic he feels his heart smash violently in his chest like a relentless caged bird.

Suddenly, she fades off the screen and is gone, and Kai's cartoon-like playback of shapes and tones continues to blush and dye without the twirls of the girl with a tail and then with legs. And all is calm. His patterns roll on.

But now, these patterns of Kai's are bleeding into Victor's. The resolver shakes his head – *this isn't normal*. But he doesn't want to worry the royals. 'Perfectly normal,' he reassures the parents with a lie. The projections aren't meant to grab at one another like this – shift, emulate, tango like a game of shadow puppets. Their colours, at times, are synchronised, they move in time. 'Impossible,' the resolver mutters to himself as the projections imitate one another, battle, play tag.

The Mer have never seen anything like it. Sienna holds her nerve, already frazzled from the day's events. This only makes things more curious, and then, when things can't get any more unusual, the Lorali silhouette skips onto the projection of Victor. The crowd make a fuss.

Lots of 'Isn't that . . . ?'

'Wasn't that . . . ?'

'She looks just like the princess . . .'

But the resolver asks for silence. *Does this mean they know one another? Is there something they are not telling the resolver?* Myrtle shuffles in her seat, frowning in confusion. Ruffles of gossip scatter across the crowd. Even the boys, virgins to tapestry reading, know this is strange; they can't help but glance at each other, nervously, from the exposed podiums where they lie. It's Victor who sees it first. Senses it.

Do they know each other? Do they share a friend? A lover? Did they fight? Are they enemies? Are they . . .

And Victor's skin suddenly begins to transform. Becomes camouflaged in tattoos. Elaborate patterns and colours on his

277

skin, like tracing paper. Of maps and words and lines of poetry. Of constellations. Of animals and beasts. Birds. Of hearts. Of planets and ships and anchors. Of a mother who never loved him. Of a boat named *Liberty*. The names of his brothers inked for ever onto his skin . . .

And Victor remembers. These stories reveal themselves, clues to truth hidden within the eternal diary that he wore tattooed onto his own flesh. The word *Ablegare* and the words *brothers with no mothers* provoke something deep.

This tapestry that he wore even as a Walker. Before he knew the real me. He isn't sure what the patterns mean exactly, as I stole his memory, but he trusts his instinct.

He is right to.

He cannot help himself.

He rips his body up from the white rock, just as Lorali did those years before. He cannot resolve to Sienna.

He owes it to himself.

He would rather die.

And over the sound of the crowd screaming, Sienna wants to roar in humiliation and anger as her only salvaged darts off. Tearing away from her; but she holds a smile. Firm.

And just as she is about to go after him, her chain begins to pull . . .

Tight. Tight. Tighter. Rattle. Rattle. Rattle . . . She is almost dragged to the ground. Is it Nevermind? Has she done her work? Why does it seem she is coming closer? Why is she not heading back to her cell? Sienna tries to hold the smile but it is undeniable: her cuff is dragging her down . . .

Something is at the other end of it and it is coming.

AURABEL

THE CHAIN

Once I know she's clocked me, I drop the other end of the chain to the ground. 'Oi, Sienna!' It feels amazing to say her name but my voice is so nervous, I have to lock myself in, be somebody new, as everybody turns to face us. I drop the other end of the chain to the ground. The adrenaline rushing through my veins is so intense, like I could chuck up any second, and my voice sounds well different. Proper large and taking up all the space.

Sienna goes cold. Scaredy-catfish, she is. Frozen right there. I see her flinch for a moment but then it's nothing a twitch of the mouth won't sort, a readjustment of the posture. Anything to not lose face. Shitty habit to never be genuine; winds me right up.

I can't help myself.

I step further in now. Into sight. Revealing my full self properly. That's when I hear them all. Talking about me. I must be quite a vision. Bit of a shock. My body: machine and iron. My shaved head. My definition. I reckon every bit of me looks different. My eye colour. My expression as they begin to realise who I am. I feel like the hugest thing in the universe.

I can see my Tips.

Zar, the king. The council.

That boy from the palace. Completely forgot about ever meeting him that day. He's strapped to the rock. All bound up. It must be his resolution. Poor sod. Resolving in a time like this. To a king like him. But watching him watching me gives me strength.

I'm so close now. 'SIENNA!' Proper top of my fucking lungs like I'm gonna blow down some mountain ship with the ripping burn of my voice. 'SIENNA!' I rip. And now she knows she can't avoid me. Knows I've got her serpents under a leash. Cos I have. Under my fucking command. Her own beasts hissing against *her* with their new metal body parts. We've done 'em up well nice, given them helmets and mended all their injuries (from my doing) with metal patches. They've even got muzzles – which I won't be using right about now.

The other Mer start gawping and shrieking at me. Like they've seen a ghost. Back from the dead. Or maybe thinking I'm about to set these pesky serps off on them. They don't all recognise me. To them, I am someone new. To me, I *am* someone new. With black blood running through me. This is what torture does.

'I'm sorry?' Sienna tries to give it the big show, doesn't she? The whole Whirl mutes to a crispy silence. Sienna's trying to orchestrate the thing, now – nah! 'Why do you have my chain?' She talks to me like I'm the scum of the Whirl.

I stay quiet.

She tries again at me. 'Where is Nevermind?' *Nope.* I stay silent. *Stubborn. Victorious.* 'Do I *know* you?' She looks at me like I'm an urchin caught on the flip of her tail, her voice all sarcastic and fake like some crook.

The king, Zar, raises his trident to me now, ready to hunt me. Kill me. Imprison me. I hear him warn me but I don't listen and continue on as planned; I'm already dead to them, see . . . I don't give a fuck now.

'Oh, you don't remember me?' I volunteer. 'No?' Holding the monsters steady just as much as my own nerve. 'Don't remember no girl from Tippi, no?'

I hear Tips gasp. I see my friends in the crowd. The Mer I love and miss. They begin to call my name.

'AURABEL!'

'AURABEL!'

'AURABEL!'

Six, five, four, three, two . . .

They cry out for me. I can't see Murray but my eyes keep trying to find her. It's breaking my focus. *Where is she?* No. Mustn't let her soften me; stay strong before I can even glance her way.

'Funny that. Don't remember how you convinced me that the king was an awful chap for sending me out all alone on my first day?'

The Mer from Tippi choke on this, as I blow a hurricane of shock across the water. I can see the king out the corner

281

of my eye lowering his staff, looking to Keppel. *Confused.*
Betrayed.

Sienna looks small. Algae-like. She stumbles but catches her
boldness with a pick; plucking on the strings of a threatening
sentence she says, 'I don't recall ever saying such a thing – nor
you for that matter, I'm afraid. You may well be the missing
Tippi girl but, I'm sorry, I'm not going to be your *pathetic*
cover story to explain why you've been gone all this time.'
Her tongue whips as she lies, splitting in two. 'Now you've
interrupted a royal resolution with your terrible manners, which
is an offence. I can't say I'm surprised. It's what I expect from
a *Tip*.' The Tips begin to bellow and roar at Sienna, booing
her. 'Why not go back where you came from before you dig
yourself any deeper?'

'HA! No chance!' I howl. How I've longed to see her
miserable face. 'I wanna see if you remember me.' My Tips know
me. They *know* me. They shout my name, louder and louder.
They recognise me. Even with my bloody bald moon-head
and box-square shoulders; even with my streamlined jaw and
eyes full of hate. Even with my metal tail. I continue. My eyes
locked. My stance proud. 'Don't remember sending me to
die with these beasts? No? Ordering them to *get* me, kill me,
eat me? For your own benefit? Then lying about it? To ruin
the king? These beasts that once *served* you?' Sienna looks to
the king, almost like she wants him to drive his fork into my
chest – but no, he doesn't; he wants to hear more.

I hear the king mutter my name as he realises who I am.
That little over-excitable girl from Tippi town who never came
home again.

I remain. Angrily huge. Monstrous. With the beasts at my side, snarling, all gnarly, hatefully growling at their master.

'I wonder . . .' I scratch my bald head with my free hand, the other one looped around the beasts. 'Perhaps someone else might jog your memory. Someone who is a much better talker than me.'

Lorali

HOME

I reveal myself. Shaking. I don't think I'm about to even breathe, let alone *talk*.

I hear my name but it doesn't sound like mine. Not now. Not any more. *Mother. Father.* Hold tight. Breathe in. Cry. I can't do anything as we planned. I can't do anything except fall into them. Eyes rummage me.

'Your chest? What happened?' I feel their fingers on my heart, line the weave of blue hair, but I can't even say through all the tears. They thought I was dead. They thought I was gone.

'It's true, Father, everything she is saying. Sienna saw me. She saw me fall.'

My father's face contorts. Anger storms over his eyes, his mouth, his brows. He knows I am telling the truth. But Sienna fights back.

'LIARS!' she blows. 'They are liars! As if you are going to believe what these deluded strangers are conjuring up. They have lived in isolation; we do not know them any –'

'You told me my daughter was DEAD!'

'Now, those weren't my *exact* words, Zar . . .' And Sienna begins to grovel, cowering into the corner, her own serpent beasts hissing and stirring at her waist. 'I'm sorry – I had no choice. I didn't mean it; I didn't mean it. I was doing it for the greater good. Tippi? Mer of Tippi? Tips, please, this is not what it looks like, please.' She tries again as my father's trident presses into the soft white flesh of her neck. 'You are an *amazing* king. Thank you for this authority; I think you are very brave and very, very good at your job. In fact, you've really improved since we last spoke; have you –'

And it's Myrtle who handles Sienna directly, pinning her arms into cuffs behind her back. Guards wade her away, Keppel's narwhals trailing behind, tusks angrily clanking . . . Sienna, begging for her life. Howling. Her screams rattle my bones.

And there he is.

I see him.

I see him see me.

Like putting a hand to a flame, I reach forward. Like petting a nervous animal. He sits up. He is shaking. Nervous . . . I see that the other boy got away. But Rory . . . he is different . . . he has a tapestry. He has a tail. A beautiful one of colour and light.

My brain begins to join dots. No.

'Did my parents salvage you?'

He nods. 'Zar found me.'

I cry. I cry so hard. My body aching. From time and loss and missing so much. From desperation. From exhaustion. And how crossed we were and still are. Fate, our aching thorn.

285

'I never thought I'd see you again.' I touch his face; his long hair falls about my hands. 'I can't believe that I am seeing you again.'

We shift together, clumsy at first, trying to re-establish, settle in. Elementary; touch is a fragile game. You make me. Embrace, holding tightly, chests fixing to one another. I don't care who sees me. *I know you. You know me.* So long I've waited to feel. Hold tight. It's all too close. Too warm. Lips. Neck. Hands. Forget everything. Forget everybody. *Does he know me? Does he know me the way I know him?*

I can't stop staring my eyes into his and touching his face and his hands and his bullet wound but he is looking back at me, trying to learn me again, trying to make sense. He shakes his head. He closes his eyes. He looks for Carmine and she nods. He looks up again. Right at me. Dead close and the foggy world soaks away.

What do you feel, Kai?

His eyes are simple black hoops that look at me with nothing to say. Empty. They twitch. And then suddenly his tapestry begins to morph and speak to me . . .

It paints Hastings. England. Football. The kind eyes of Cheryl. Flynn. Iris. The lighthouse.

Fish and chips.

Pickled onions in jars like glass eyeballs.

Of his dad. Spain. Pirates. Birds. The sea. And projected onto the scales is a shadow: a silhouette of a girl.

A girl. *And the girl is me.*

'I remember,' he says. 'I remember Lorali.'

But . . . I can't . . . I scramble . . . for air, can't breathe, tight chest and choking. Gasp for air. Not now. Why now? Swallowing

286

it. Sucking it up. Eyes panic. Keppel. Zar. His face falls. He shakes me. Holds my throat. Rory tries to help me. They call him *Kai*. NO! It's Rory! Rory! His name is RORY! All the Mer come forward, touch me. *Hands off! Get off.* I hold my throat. Too many eyes. Hands. Voices. Starving me. Heavy. Small. Tight. Gulp. Light-headed, I fall. Backwards. Rory has me in his arms as the weight on my chest presses harder and harder and the little spirit of air within me has gone.

THE SEA

SOLVE

Aurabel, already there, right there on the white rock. Pressing down with open palms on her ribs. Blowing air into her mouth. She begins to unpick Lorali's stitches, whilst Keppel wrestles with the girl's working hands, but Aurabel reassures her that it is what has to happen. Blood crawls out like rumours – dancing, whispering away. Kai begins to cry. Memories rolling back into his brain.

Rory. It is me. I am Rory and you are Lorali.

Reels of blood-stained blue hair fray away. The chest, an open mouth, and out come the metal lungs. One and two. Mer gasp. They've never seen anything like this before. Eyes together. Holding. Blocking out the world. Silence casts a spell of mourning. Long heavy tears slide and spill. Hands hold. Moved and hopeful. The blue princess sleeping, quiet and still on the same white rock she left from all those moons ago. Concentrating, ignoring the voices, Aurabel engineers, using tools from her tail, sacrificing her own spare scrap to repair what has been broken.

Aurabel threads her blue hair into her friend's skin. Joining flesh together and, as the reflection of the light rebounds from the rock, Lorali's eyes meet Aurabel's as she wakes. Her tapestry finally morphs. Lorali at last resolves. A beautiful history paints itself onto the canvas of her skin. A shining, detailed, strong tapestry that steals the Mer's breath. Speaking of happiness. Of the grass, the pebbles on the beach, salt on her tongue, sun in her eyes, music in her ears, the stars in the sky, the sound of laughter, the touch of flesh, the heat, the sting, the sequence of a day, the change of a season, the smile of a child, the kindness in a stranger, the architecture of a building, the bliss of a belly laugh, the taste of a lemon.

Lorali

PATCHWORK

I knew Murray would be pretty. But I never expected her to be this pretty. You can know a love but love is a rich tapestry that has many layers. It is never as simple as it seems.

It was Victor who found her, locked in Sienna's chamber. Red eyes, sore and angry; broken fingers; ripped flesh from fighting the iron claw bolting her in.

She was clutching the papery patchwork of her girl's tail. Sick. Heartbroken and sorry.

He only wrapped his arms around Murray and told her that he kept his promise. That everything is going to be OK. And this time, it would be.

Aurabel. A new Mer. Shaved head. Big. Half metal. Covered in wounds and bruises and scars like an old banana at the bottom of a bag. Still, as always, she is Murray's girl. It's in the hands. The skin. The voice. The reason. The feeling that lets you know. Even when two paths spindle off, it doesn't mean they aren't going to meet up, once again, somewhere along the way towards the end.

And sometimes, there doesn't have to be words all getting in the way. Sometimes we owe it to the patchwork of our own tapestries to say what we don't have to. Some threads are too deep and thick to fray.

Some lines, in love, outlive the veins.

THE SEA

EPILOGUE

Above water, it is a surprising day for Walkers. Hundreds of beautiful naked women crawl out of the water and onto the shores. They are hungry and cold without their skins but it doesn't take them long to find new homes.

With frowned, concerned faces, Cheryl and Flynn sit by Iris's bedside. His sickness has spun him to a wintery flour-white. He sinks in the dregs of a hospital bed. Lino floor and ticking clock. Wilting purple petals in gunky water. Plastic cups and soggy greens. The babble of daytime TV. Chalky bitter tablets and the yellowing wires of fluid. 'Flynn, my grandson,' he softly crackles as his wavering heartbeat drops. 'I have a fairly small favour to ask.'

Another moon counted in the square of Tippi. The newly appointed mayor of Tippi, Victor, stands proud. Later he will join his best friend, Kai, for drinks and games at the palace . . . He's met a Tip. Her name: Orina.

Across the way, as the light shifts from blue navy night to

the sweet cream of dawn, we see a happy Nevermind, freely dozing under my waves.

A dirty long grey chain, heavy and gruelling, joins Sienna to the wall of a cell. She rots in the pit, under the Sabre Tower. Powerless, friendless and probably remorseless. She is history forgotten.

At the council meeting, Carmine is late, as usual . . . but Myrtle, Keppel, Zar and a new member, Aurabel, are planning a hearing. They have exciting news. Lorali is to be queen and Kai king. For the first time in the Whirl it is decided that the best things come in twos. A balanced, equal set of scales.

Carmine finally rushes up in a hysterical fluster. 'I'm sorry I'm late,' she squeals excitedly as she rejoins the meeting. 'I've done it!' she shrieks. 'I've salvaged.' And over her shoulder she carries the body of a man she has loved all her life, a man she has waited for. His heart strong, there's so much to see for this all-seeing Iris, in this all-seeing sea.

One day, a way away, Flynn will walk his own little ones over a pebble beach. The sound of laughter and my waves pushing in and pushing out. I will keep low and let him know it is safe. He might follow the springing leaps of his children towards the petrified forest. They will play hide and seek and hunt and fish. And he will tell them all about the qualities of the forest and how it sinks itself and then reveals.

'Why does it have to disappear?' the youngest will ask.

'It doesn't disappear,' Flynn will tell them. 'It just leaves for a little while. The world is round for a reason,' he will say.

Nobody, ever, really has to leave.

Acknowledgements

Thank you, Jenny, for editing *Aurabel* with me and encouraging me to write a follow up to *Lorali* (there very nearly wasn't one!). Thank you for pushing me when needed, punishing me when needed and praising me when REALLY needed. You are a tremendous editor and an even better teacher, thank you for your guidance.

Thank you to Catherine for the copy-edit.

Thank you to my agents at United: Jodie, Emily, Jane and Dan.

Thank you to all at Hot Key/Bonnier for their support and faith in this book. In particular, Emma, Tina and Jane.

Thanks to Alex for the potato-print cover design.

Thank you to Jen, Rosi and Sanne for their amazing ideas and getting up at the crack of dawn to sail on a floating house with me.

Thank you to Sarah.

Thank you to all of the readers of *Lorali*.

Thank you to my friends and family.

Laura Dockrill

Laura Dockrill is a performance poet and novelist whose wonderfully inventive and creative approach to life is reflected in the rich and vividly imagined worlds she creates. Laura lives in London, and you can follow her on Twitter @LauraDockrill

Want to read
NEW BOOKS
before anyone else?

Like getting
FREE BOOKS?

Enjoy sharing your
OPINIONS?

Discover

READERS
FIRST

Read. Love. Share.

Get your first free book just by signing up at
readersfirst.co.uk